Him, Her & that Secret

AJ. Underwhite

Authors note
Thank you to all that contributed,
unknowingly.

A.J.Underwhite.

The grass will always be green.

Present

Alora

Looking down from above, I observe the doctors and nurses rushing around me frantically with pumps and resuscitation equipment. I feel an unusual sense of calm as I admire the determination of those frantically trying to save my life. One by one I watch those that are ushered out of the room away from me until I allow my eyes to wander onto myself. I look peaceful, relaxed, and calm, as if I am merely asleep and enjoying a wonderful dream. I feel nothing, no anger, no strength, no physical pain, no emotion, no resentment, no wondering why I am a here, no regrets, no sadness, no love, no more thinking about the love affair as I slowly and calmy drift into a beautiful and peaceful sleep.

Alora and Blake, Sadie and Lucian, Cassy and Kyle, three couples, all 'friends,' one illicit love affair, which led to the happenings of the present.

Fate

The Driver

The decision to run and leave Alora, is one that I will regret for the rest of my life.

Life is full of decisions we make them every day, some big some not so. Tea or coffee? Stay or go? I chose the latter. I am not entirely heartless, I waited until she had received the help that she needed. I did seek help and I did tell the middle-aged lady walking her dog, that she needed to ring an ambulance as soon as possible. I couldn't tell you what breed of dog she had. In that split second that I decided to run, and as quickly as my mind was made up, it was still the hardest decision that I have ever had, or perhaps will ever make. Yes, I lied to the lady about not having a phone, but I needed to protect Alora. She is the love of my life and always will be. I was able to hide until the ambulance arrived, but it was at that moment that my heart was fighting hard with my head the most. That was my biggest battle. It still is.

As I sit here now hiding in the woods at the side of the embankment, my heart is still racing, my hands are still shaking and I realise it is not too late. The traffic is heavy to the right of me, the peacefulness of the woods leading to the lake to my left. I envy the squirrel running up the tree, running away but still finding safety at the top of it. I stare at the tree for a while, it's an old oak. I stare so hard until I find its face looking back at me. Is it judging me? I wonder how many secrets that old oak tree had held in its ancient years. I wonder how old it is and how much it has seen in its ancient life. Suddenly the face looking back at me from the tree is no longer baring its own face, it is Alora's.

The affair

Within seconds of him answering the front door, she knew that she may give in. *'It is going to be hard, hopefully it's not.'* His eyes are smiling along with his pleasing mouth. The palm of his hand open in a directional and welcoming manner to enter his house.

She hears her rehearsed speech that she has mentally repeated to herself in her head, all day.

'I'm sorry, this can't go on anymore, it's over as of now and I am not coming in tonight.'

She lifts herself up to the top step on his doorstep and takes a deep breath. It is too late. He is not even discreet. He pulls her body towards him as if he knew what she has been rehearsing all day. She enters his hallway, just for him to at least close the front door, her back is up against the hall wall. His warm hands undoing her bra, before she can resist he is pushed up against her. The buttoned-up silk blouse she purposely wore now completely open. As his mouth caresses her neck, he takes off his shirt baring his manly chest as she finds herself wearing nothing but her black lacy underwear. Within minutes she had given in to temptation.

'No, no, no, had dominated her voice into yes, yes, yes.

'This was not meant to happen. Not tonight. I was here to end it, for good this time.'

Her

At the seaside, many years ago, a fortune teller told me that my love life would be complicated. My friend laughed so hard at the time, she was very sceptical of the fortune teller's 'bullshit advice' as she called it, and parting with her fifteen pound didn't appeal to her either. Cautiously, she let me go in first and then completely changed her mind and didn't go in at all. The fortune teller told me I would hurt a friend, that part I kept to myself. She did not say which friend, although I didn't have many at the time. She also did not tell me that the same friend would hurt me either.

Everyone has a story left untold, usually because their fear of being judged. Usually there are three sides to the love story, his, hers and the truth. I never say never because limits like fears, are often just an illusion.

As for the hurt I have caused I wish I could explain it, but I cannot.

Him

No comment.

Chapter One

Present - Alora

I could not recall how I had arrived at this beautiful place, that bright light that I had heard people talk about with their 'near death' experience had guided me through a tunnel to the openness of the electric blue of the sky. The speed at which I had travelled, was a strange combination of very fast and very slow. The alluring blue sky, appeared to be so high above me, yet it was almost touching my skin, until I could feel it's positive energy.

A stern middle-aged lady stood at the entrance of a large gate, holding a sign, with her eyes directed onto me. I felt myself uncontrollably moving towards her. The sign read 'Heaven only' and I burst into a fit of giggles, much to the stern lady's annoyance. I felt younger, almost childlike, carefree, and irresponsible.

'Do I have a choice?' I asked the stern lady dressed in some kind of security uniform that reminded me of a matron's uniform that I had seen in old pictures of my grandmother. The stern lady looked me up and down before replying. 'Yes of course, that is why you are here, you can either enter or you can go back to where you came from, or you stay here for a while until you make your decision, so if you are not sure, could you please do the latter as it looks like we are pretty busy this evening.'

My giggles at her matter-of-fact tone suddenly halted as a bright light pulled me with a force of energy, like a full breeze at a speed. I travelled past the stern lady and through a tunnel which guided me over a beautiful bridge. I perched myself onto a large rock, and my eyes were drawn to the most beautiful beach I had ever seen with the sea and sky an exact match of blue azure.

I stretched out to perform a cartwheel in the sand, and my body felt free of any pain as I dared to run and somersault like I was fourteen years old again, in which I completed proudly with a perfect landing.

The distance appeared to be moving towards me as the ant like animal objects were becoming larger and clearer. A four-legged animal started running towards me at a profound speed, and as my eyes widened I found myself calling **'Hugo!'** and there he was my lovely little Hugo, his full force knocking me off balance until I was laying backwards on the beautiful sand as I had welcomed him onto my lap and let him lick my cheeks playfully and lovingly.

Hugo was my pet husky dog from when I was nine years old until I was twenty-two. His coat was still as beautiful with its white and grey colours accompanying his little wolf like face. My heart broke the day that he died, one day after my birthday. I knew he was determined to selflessly let me enjoy my birthday before he passed away. As I hugged him, a beautiful rainbow appeared from nowhere and that is when I came to the realisation that I was on 'Rainbow Bridge.'

Blake, drove straight to the hospital as soon as he received the message regarding Alora's accident, it was 7.20pm and he needed to get to the centre of London. He felt sick, his beloved Alora, the love of his life, he wanted to be with her, he needed to be with her, and *she* needed *him*. He finally arrived at the car park next to the accident and emergency department, in his haste he left his car without purchasing a ticket and tried to be as patient as he could be as he waited at the reception desk, where the receptionist appeared to be in no rush. A woman holding a crying toddler stood in front of him. He couldn't wait and rushed past them through the automatic doors to try and find Alora. His haste was noted by the security guard who raced towards him and caught up with him. Blake approached a petite nurse with red hair of whom he recognised from before when he had visited his friend. He gave her Alora's name impatiently but politely. As she cradled her coat she informed Blake that she was just leaving her shift and waved her colleague over towards them. She asked Blake who he was and then took him to the side of the corridor and explained that Alora had been placed in an induced coma in intensive care. She wasn't allowed any visitors at present as she was being prepared for major surgery on her back and, Blake was told that he could wait in a side room for now.

As the nurse guided him into the side room, he was surprised to see his friend Sadie already there with Lucian, Alora's friend Cassy and her partner Kyle. Sadie ran up to Blake upon entry.

'Oh my god, this is awful, why is this happening?'

Sadie asked as she sobbed uncontrollably to an otherwise shocked silence around her as she buried her head into Blakes's chest. Her immaculate scarlet red nails were harbouring a worn-out tissue, and as she fiddled for a fresh one from the packet in her handbag, she noticed the arrival of Alora's shocked and distraught parents.

Kyle was watching Cassy, her face was pale, and her voice unusually quiet. He tried to put on a brave face and hide his own pain. Minutes later, the shocking words of the four police officers accompanying them in the waiting room were a little too much to bear for Blake, as himself, Sadie, Lucian, Cassy, and Kyle were all taken to their local police station, and within half an hour all of them separated into interview rooms for questioning.

*

The affair

Her

'I'm going!' She shouted as she slammed the front door behind her.

Him

'Hey you ok? What's going on with you two?'

Her

'No not really, sorry she has really annoyed me, I know she's your girlfriend, but she can be bloody hard work at times!'

Her

'Well, I know that, but come on you two are mates, can't you sort it out? Why don't you come back in?'

Her

'No, not tonight she's had too much to drink and so have I and well, I will probably speak to her tomorrow or something.'

Him

'Okay, but what are you going to do walk home? Shall I call you a cab?'

Her

'I just called one but it's an hour wait and well, it's fine honestly I'll walk, thanks.'

Him

'Well, it's a bit cold and late and look, give me a minute and I will drive you; I'll just go in and see her for a minute.'

Her

'Okay, thank you, if you're sure you don't mind? But I will wait here on the drive for you.'

Him

'She's gone to bed, I told her I will give you a lift home.'

Her

'Thank you.'

Him

'So, come on what was it about, another debate? Or just tell me to mind my own business, but I'm sure she'll tell me all about it in the morning.'

Her

'Yep.'

Him

'Haha, is that all you are going to give me?'

Her

'Sorry, but yeah.'

Him

'Is that it?'

Her

'Put it this way, let's just say we have different morals!'

Him

'O-kay, I'll say no more and for the…shit, what's happening gears are stuck, no power, fuck I need to pull over, hang on bloody car, it's new!'

Her

'Oh no sorry, not your night tonight is it.'

The bright shining light had reappeared, and Alora was flowing back through the tunnel at a speed, passing the stern lady again, her body flowing freely yet with force, until she found herself in the most beautiful garden she had ever seen amongst an array of one of her favourite flowers, cherry blossom, she soon realised she was seated underneath the prettiest pink cherry blossom tree amongst the expanse of green, orange and gold.

To the right side of her, an ever-lasting bed of marigolds lay. To the left of her lay a never-ending azure of blue, including geranium and hydrangea, and in front, lay a beautiful array of every colour. She inhaled the beautiful aroma around her, and her eyes were drawn to one of her favourite red flowers dahlia, she smiled and closed her eyes until she felt the warm hand of the nurse on hers.

'Hello dear.'

Alora suddenly saw a flash of the car accident and the black car that had hit her. She squeezed her eyes closed, and could hear a lady talking to her, on reopening her eyes, she found her vision to be slightly blurred. She could not feel a thing physically and her thoughts suddenly turned to Blake as she quietly mouthed his name. 'There's lot of Blake's here, you can have your pick of Blakes pet. You have entered a new life now love, you are in between your previous life and the afterlife, I don't think you can make you mind up at the moment, but when you are ready pet, try and get up and make yourself at home.'

Alora looked at the nurse quizzically and then let her

eyes wander around the room. She soon realised that she was no longer in the hospital back home anymore, in fact she wasn't in a hospital or a room, unless it was a never-ending room. In fact, the lady was no longer in a nurse's uniform. The lady also looked remarkably familiar to her. She was a cuddly lady whom Alora felt an instant comfort and warmth from and as her eyes came into focus the identity of this lady became clear.

'Are you going to give your great aunt Ede a hug then or what?'

Alora shot up straight, her body was in fine form. No pain, no aches, no knee pain that she had been suffering from for months she thought happily as she felt the warm hug from her Great Aunt Ede that had passed three years ago. Alora could almost taste the pleasant familiar aroma of vanilla from her.

'Aunt Ede, have I died?'

'You have temporarily passed my dear,' Aunt Ede said softly comforting Alora in her short but secure strong arms.

'There is no such thing as dying, just passing to another part of life, you needed a break from your troubles, which is why you are here. Now start from the beginning and tell me all about it, tell me about you and Blake.'

'How do you know about Blake Aunt Ede?'

'Because when you have troubles I look down on you and try to guide you, I don't know every detail though, but you needed a break, so here you are pet.'

The affair

Her

She awoke the morning after that kiss and felt awful. Awful for her behaviour, awful because of his behaviour, and awful for her friend. 'What had she been thinking?' She sighed as she rubbed her fingers through her hair. Clearly she hadn't. She started to message him.

'Hey, I'm so sorry about last night..' She deleted it.

'Are you okay' She deleted that too. She would try and blank it out of her mind and pretend it hadn't happened, maybe that was the answer, and hopefully he would blank it out of his mind too. That is exactly what she did for the rest of the day, until her 'friend' the one she had betrayed messaged her at 6.42pm.

'Hey, how's you after last night? Sorry I was in a funny one, plus I have just come on my period, u know what I'm like lol.. peace offering virtual hug ( ) xx

A wave of guilt washed over her.

'I know you have probably got plans now but I am on my own tonight, the other half is in a weird one, he has been since yesterday, so we are not really speaking, anyway, do you fancy popping round, start last night all over again?'

'?'

'Hey, no worries, sorry I'm feeling a bit rough myself, yeah we are cool and I'm going to have a long hot soak. Hope you both sort it. Xx'

Him

'You did what?'

'I know, it was stupid.'

'You said it mate, but then again I suppose you are both even now aren't..' There was a paused silence for a moment as his friend soon realised he had spoken without thinking.

'What do you mean?'

'Ah nothing I didn't mean....'

'No, what do you mean? 'you're even now' what do you mean?'

'Look I don't know; it might be something and nothing. I saw her, the other week, I was driving past yours when I was diverted, remember when there was that road closed It was late and she was in a car with someone, she leant over and gave whoever it was a kiss, I just thought it was a mate or something, but it was definitely her. I had to stop at traffic lights, so I looked in my rear-view mirror as they weren't parked directly outside your house, it was near the bottom of the road near the junction. Thought it was odd but....'

'And you never thought to tell me this?'

'Well, you know what she's like with all her contacts and I thought it was her brother at first and because of the diversion and the temporary lights and ..'

'And the kiss was not just a pec then?'

'Honestly? no, I don't think so mate.'

Chapter Two

The Investigation

Alora had been involved in a head on collision with one other driver and had sustained a spinal injury and was currently recovering from emergency surgery on her back and was now resting in an induced coma. The other driver had left the scene instantly on foot. The vehicle involved had been traced to one of Sadie's husband Lucian's hire vehicles, in which Sadie, Lucian and Cassy all had access to keys too and now Blake, Sadie, Lucian, Kyle and Cassy were all about to be interviewed.

So, when was the last time you saw Alora? apart from this evening at the hospital?' Jenkins, the Detective Superintendent asked Sadie, ignoring her crying.

'Erm,' Sadie was distracted by the policewoman's rather large mole on her face momentarily, 'at the weekend we had a barbeque at my house, mine and my boyfriend Lucian's house. Why are you asking me these questions? I should be there at the hospital; we all should be!' Sadie's question was ignored by the stern looking middle aged hard faced female officer, she had very sharp features and was squinting her unusually small eyes at Sadie, almost as if she had already made her mind up that Sadie had something to do with Alora's accident.

'So, you didn't see Alora at all today, prior to the accident?' Detective Wilson asked. Wilson was a little more patient than Jenkins, he could see that his colleague was getting impatient with Sadie's sobbing and passed her a box of tissues. In Jenkins thirty-five-year experience, Sadie's hysterical sobbing could potentially be a sure sign of guilt.

'No, I told you, I have been busy today at work and then, after work, I collected my daughter Amelia from the child carer and was just about to drive home to meet Lucian when I received the call about Alora.'

'So where is Amelia now? How old is she, and what's your child carers name?' Jenkins asked suspiciously.

'She is with Natalia, she's our child carer, Amelia is with her, she is only three, that's why I have to get back and pick her up from *her* house.' Jenkins decided to let Sadie make a phone call to her childcare worker to check on her daughter, then proceeded with the interview.

Blake was next in line for questioning and Detective Superintendent Wilson, took the lead this time. At just less than under three years' experience than Jenkins, he held a different approach to her when interviewing. Jenkins always assumed guilt, which Wilson believed could perhaps be damaging to their suggestive subjects, if they had any suspicion that they were no to be believed by the officer in question. Wilson was a little more unassuming than Jenkins and liked to gather all the facts and evidence first. His calm but firm and objective approach had sometimes proven to have a more reliable and successful outcome, which had been slightly resented by Jenkins at times; however, both did have outstanding track records and either one of them, if not both would eventually find out the truth.

Blake appeared to be in a slight daze and was clearly still in a state of shock, Wilson noted and proceeded in his gentle approach to earn his trust.

'So, Blake, Alora is your girlfriend, is this correct?' Blake hesitated slightly, 'yes.'

'So I understand this may be hard for you and I appreciate that you would like to be by her side, but I do know she is resting at the moment after her surgery and there is little you would be able to do at the hospital this evening, so we need to do our job to try and find out who the other driver is.'

Blake took an inward breath of slight relief at the fact that Alora's surgery had been a success. He knew she was going to be having major surgery on her spine, but to hear it had been a success was gratifying.

'So, all questions I ask, will help us find the other driver involved.' Blake gave a quick nod of appreciation.

'Can I ask you Blake how long you and Alora have been together?'

'Er, four maybe five years now I think?'

'And you live together?'

'No.'

'No children?'

Blake's face saddened. 'Unfortunately, no.'

'Your choice? Her choice? A mutual agreement?'

Blake rubbed his face in an agitated way.

'What has this got to do with it?' Blake snapped as Wilson tilted his head to the right and waited patiently for his answer.

'Sorry,' Blake apologised lowering his voice back down again, 'It's just not happened yet. Alora wants to be a mum of course she does.' Wilson nodded as he sensed the tension around the subject.

'And you and Alora, your relationship, would you say you were both… happy?'

Blake looked down to the right of him hesitantly, Wilson knew the answer before Blake had replied.

'Yes I am happy, we are happy, I'm not happy now I just want to see Alora please I know you have a job to do but please, she needs me I was working late, I should have been there with her and …'

'Ok, we'll take five minutes would you like a drink?'

'Yes please.'

Lucian sat down in a very professional business-like manner as if he was about to close a business deal. *'Very cool and calm,'* Jenkins's thought, in her experience this calm approach could often potentially lead to guilt. She was hoping that he would reveal more than his hysterical girlfriend Sadie had, she wasn't so sure now. After her initial questions and after Lucian had listed every single person that had access to his business and to the car that had been involved in the accident, she wanted to paint a larger picture, plus Sadie had stated that Lucian was closer to Alora than Sadie was because they had apparently shared some 'history.'

'So, Lucian you say you have known Alora for roughly five years, and you met when Cassy, her friend started working for you is that correct?'

'Yes.'

'And you and Alora?' *'Here we go,'* Lucian thought, he was waiting for this, and this could have only come from Sadie.

'Have you ever had more than a friendship; you know in a romantic way at all?'

'No comment.'

'Interesting' thought Wilson, Lucian's only 'no comment' answer.

Blake was trying to hide the tremble of both his hands while he sipped his coffee as Wilson waited patiently.

'So, Blake, the last time you saw Alora, when was that please?'

'Saturday.'

'And where was that?'

'At my friend Sadie's, Lucian's and Sadie's house they had a barbeque.' Blake replied as he swilled the plastic coffee cup around as if to disguise his trembling hands.

'Okay so you and Alora you live separately?' Blake paused before he replied.

'Yes,' he said quietly, 'at the moment yes.'

'And you and Alora, married, engaged?'

'No.'

'You don't live together?' Jenkins asked. Blake stared at the large mole on Jenkins's face subconsciously before replying. 'We like our independence, we both do.'

'So, you and Alora were you on good terms on Saturday?' Wilson quizzed. Blake didn't reply as his mind flashed back to Saturday and all the drama.

'Yes we bickered, but don't all couples?' Blake justified.

'We have a witness stating that there was a lot of noise,' Wilson looked down at his notes, 'a lot of shouting and arguing and some physical violence' reported, which took place outside Lucian and Sadie's house on… Saturday, did this involve you and Alora?' Jenkins asked.

'No.' Blake replied. 'Look between you and me, Alora is very emotional at the moment, you know she has some emotional problems, she has been stressed at work and she can be quite fiery and sometimes you know, when alcohol is consumed she can just start arguing for no reason, but I support her and take care of her as much as I can and like her mother will tell you, I have a very calming influence on her.'

'So,' Jenkins asked the same question again, 'did this arguing and violence that was reported by a neighbour outside number twenty-one on Saturday involve either you or Alora?' Blake sighed as he fiddled with the ridge of indentation on his wedding finger. 'She did have an argument with Sadie, I can't even remember what it was about, it was something and nothing, but she was crying, and I just put it down to the alcohol..'

'So, what was the argument about Blake? Wilson queried.

'Nothing.' Blake replied.

'Okay….did you take Alora home after you consoled her, assuming you did?' Wilson asked.

'No, she was going somewhere after.'

'So did she leave the barbeque before you?'

'Yes, I mean no, we left at the same time ish, well maybe I left a couple of minutes before her.'

'And you say that was the last time you saw her up until you saw her in the hospital tonight, for the benefit of the tape, that's three days ago?'

'Correct.' Blake answered.

As Cassy entered the room, Wilson noticed a slight wobble on her feet, he knew that it wasn't just because she was wearing high heels, she had clearly been consuming alcohol. She was aware that it didn't look good and tried her best to hide the fact as she was seated. Her eyes were red maybe from crying, but also from the alcohol. Wilson offered her a coffee, she accepted.

'So, are you ok? Cassy or Cassandra?' Cassy let out a nervous giggle and turned to look at the duty solicitor, for his approval, which was ignored.

'Just Cassy thanks.' She laughed again. Cassy recalled a time when she was younger and whenever she started a new school, she would pretend that her mother was a queen from Australia and that her own name was Princess Cassandra. She would try and make her new friends treat her like a princess to get what she wanted.

Wilson nodded and waited for Cassy to finish her sip of coffee. As she pushed her hair away from the front of her face he noticed a red mark on the left side of her cheek.

As soon as Cassy realised this she quickly covered it with her hand while her elbow rested on the table.

'How did you hurt your face Cassy? For the benefit of the tape, Cassy has a recent injury to the left side of her face just above her cheek bone.'

'I, erm banged it at the hospital in the toilets on the hand drying machine.'

'Plausible,' Wilson thought, considering her obvious alcohol consumption, however guilt was written all over her face and she was not particularly good at lying.

'Did you see Alora at any point today?'

'No, I saw her at the weekend at Sadie's and Lucian's house at their barbeque.' Wilson paused; 'So, you have answered my next question, which was when did you see Alora last? Weekend you say, Saturday or Sunday?'

'Saturday.'

'Okay.'

Wilson proceeded with his questions regarding Cassy's friendship with Alora and more importantly Cassy's whereabouts this evening. Cassy worked in the offices for Lucian, and one of his cars had been driven by the other driver involved in the crash and as well as Lucian and Sadie, she also had access to Lucian's cars.

The interview was suddenly interrupted by a police officer, with a message of Alora's current condition of which Cassy, Wilson noted and unlike the others, had not shown any interest in. In Jenkins eyes Cassy was involved for sure.

After Cassy's interview, Wilson and Jenkins were both informed of Alora's current condition, she had recently undergone major surgery on her back and had been recovering and resting well, soon after a urine test had revealed an extremely high amount of prescription drugs in her system, and not long after, her heart rate had rapidly started to drop, and she had now been placed in an induced coma.

Kyle entered the interview room and Wilson began by asking him to confirm his relationship with Cassy, who according to Cassy was Alora's best friend.

'So, I assume you and Alora are quite well acquainted, through your girlfriend, Cassy?' Jenkins asked.

'Yes, I have known her for a while now, through Cassy, and of course, we work together at Boadfield Primary but me and…'

'Oh right, okay, sorry I didn't mean to interrupt you were saying?'

'Er yes I know Alora well.' Kyle replied while fidgeting in his chair and looking slightly uncomfortable, both Wilson and Jenkins noted. 'Okay so you and …' Wilson pauses, as if changing his mind about what he was going to say. He looks at Kyle and pauses, 'So, you and Alora being colleagues, when was the last time you saw her, other than at the hospital tonight of course?'

'The other night.'

'Okay when and where Kyle?'

'Last night, I gave her a lift to my sister's house, her car had been in the garage, and obviously I saw her at work yesterday.'

'Okay, so going back to the barbeque, at Sadie and

Lucian's house, can you recall any arguments?' Wilson noticed Kyle's hesitation.

'Kyle,' Wilson said calmy as if reading his thoughts, 'we have a woman who has been seriously hurt in a car accident, and to help us to try and put together the pieces of what has happened this evening, we have to ask all kinds of questions, they may not seem relevant to you, however they are to us. Were there any arguments on Saturday at Lucian and Sadie's house?'

Kyle thought back to Saturday, it had totally kicked off between all of them he could not possibly relay what had happened right here, right now, so he decided to play it down a little. 'The usual little argument with Sadie and Lucian, I can't even remember what it was about.' He lied; he knew full well what it was about, and all three couples had ended up in a blazing row. He also knew that Wilson was going to ask him to elaborate but was unsure of what Wilson already knew since he had spoken to the others. Kyle decided to use a petty argument that *had* actually happened earlier in the afternoon before the big argument with all of six of them, including Alora. Wilson knew there was a lot more to this 'petty argument' and would in time get to the bottom of it, eventually.

Officers had been patrolling the area and its surroundings all evening and a search was on to find the driver. Jenkins was convinced already that the driver could potentially be one of the females she had interviewed, either 'sobbing Sadie, the drama queen' or Alora's so called best friend Cassy, who had appeared to have been just a little too carefree.

Lucian, she thought, was a little too cool and calm for her liking, also and she had her suspicions of him as he had replied a 'no comment'. As for Blake he was clearly still in a state of shock and she couldn't quite put her finger on it, but she felt that Kyle was hiding something big. Wilson wasn't revealing any of his thoughts too much to Jenkins, as he preferred a slower process, he liked to interview, listen, divulge the information, think on it and sleep on it. Also, there was no fingerprint match to any of Alora's friends inside or outside of the vehicle, however as it *was* one of Lucian's cars that were used, tomorrow all of Lucian's staff would be questioned also regarding their access to the vehicle.

After a long night and with the driver still on the run reluctantly at 2.21am Jenkins and Wilson finally called it a night.

The Driver

The stars are just about to dissolve into the dawn, I wish I could, dissolve that is. Behind me is yesterday, in front of me is today. The realisation that I am no longer in the moment, and I could not possibly turn back is very hard to grasp. The last thing I wanted to happen, happened, it wasn't meant to be that way. The sound of the song from an early morning blackbird is currently my only companion. I envy the freedom of the bird. I wish I could fly away. I still have a choice. I could hand myself in, or I could keep running. I have been lucky so far, I have lied my way to this point, but I have come this far, and still my decision isn't moving towards the latter option. I hate myself for what I have done and the more I think about it the harder it is, as I watch the freedom of the wings of the birds above, the iridescent blue sky becomes the colour of my dreams.

The affair

Her

She had barely slept again last night until the early hours of the morning, her guilt had taken over last night. She had even contemplated sending her 'friend' an apology in the early hours, however this morning she had changed her mind.

'It happened and it was silly, I am going to blank it out of my mind, just like that. It was a silly kiss, emotions had been running high, I wasn't thinking straight, he wasn't thinking straight, I was stressed, he was stressed, we were both upset and that was it.

There, it was a simple as that.

I'm sure he will be doing the same, putting it down to the silly little kiss that it was.' She told herself.

She had come close to telling her 'friend' as she knew that she would want her to do the same, but after thinking it through rationally, long, and hard and convincing herself the only good that it would do, would be to ease her own guilt, she had decided against it, plus she didn't want to upset her, she had enough going on by the sounds of it. She still hadn't heard from him, she guessed he may even have forgotten all about it by now and, if he says anything, which she doubted he would, she decided that she would play it down.

Him

The thought of his partner being with another man had taken over his slight guilt of kissing her friend the other night and just added to his fury. He could even justify his behaviour if he were certain that she had been playing away. She has been busier than usual too and slightly more distant. It appeared that her friend may have been in the dark about this mystery man or she was particularly good at pretending to be. He wondered whether he should confront her, but after that silly kiss with her friend he decided not to. He would find out eventually, he would watch her carefully and if she has been playing away, then the truth would come out. Hopefully not his truth though, no, that would really mess things up. Not that things could get much worse he thought, however, on Friday night all six of them would be together at the birthday meal.

Later that evening

The Driver

'What are you doing here?'

'I know, but I don't know what to do.'

'You can't come here, I can't be seen with you, you'll have to go.'

'I just want five minutes, I may hand myself in, I don't know I..'

'Did you get the package?'

'Yes of course that's why I had to run.'

'That's something, but bloody el what a mess, are you okay anyway, are you injured?'

'I am a bit yeah, but obviously not like she is, but I hid it well, I think I did anyway. I'm so sorry…' I'm sorry for you and I'm sorry for Alora too.'

The affair

Her

'Happy Birthday to you, Happy Birthday to you, Happy Birthday dear –Happy Birthday to you. Hip hip hooray!'

He blew the candles out and made his wish to the sound of the claps and the cheers in the restaurant amongst the most bubbly, happy staff.

She felt slightly awkward as she found herself sitting directly in front of him, with his partner to the right of her and her partner to her left, oblivious. The first time the six of them had all been together since that kiss.

The guilt she suddenly felt was almost overbearing, as he caught her eye. She could barely look at him, it was so awkward, and she started to wonder if it was obvious to anyone else. After that silly kiss, she had tried to put it out of her mind, but in reality she couldn't stop thinking about him from the moment she opened her eyes until the moment she closed them at night. She had even dreamt about him last week. Her relationship at home with her partner had become a chore and a bit of a bore, they were distant, it was cold. There was no arguing, nothing. She just prayed that no one noticed both their awkwardness. The only way she would get through this evening would be to ignore him as much as she could, she decided, and then after tonight she would sort it, maybe even tell her partner and her friend. It was just a silly kiss, and it would ease her guilt and then she would work on her relationship and bring back the spark.

Him

He had tried his best to make his excuses to his partner last night to try and get out of tonight's gathering, he had tried and failed, not so miserably though as there was a tiny part of him that wanted to see her and now he was glad that he was here. Yes it was just a kiss and he had tried to forget it, but he couldn't. It had happened. Now they had to face it. He had felt a tiny bit guilty, until his mate had told him he had seen his partner getting cosy with someone else, which made him jealous, and if the truth be known there was also a part of him that had considered an open relationship, maybe it could work, it even excited him a little. Cake and eat it? Maybe.

She looked good tonight in her tight black dress, if a little uncomfortable and nervous, which he found quite endearing. Her chest went a little red when she was nervous or flustered. He found himself imagining her breasts under her V shape slightly low-cut top of her dress. The excitement of no one else knowing what had happened when he had kissed her soft full lips, turned him on a little. His partner, in her little white dress, looked good tonight too, even though she was happily flirting with one of the younger waiters, he observed. She must never know about the kiss, ever.

He justified his behaviour by convincing himself that his partner was playing away, she had certainly made more of an effort lately, new hair, new clothes, spring in her step. He picked up his phone.

'You look gorgeous tonight.'

Choice, the most powerful tool we have.

Chapter Three

'So, what's occurring?'

'Haha I haven't heard that for a while Aunt Ede, I have missed that.' Alora laughed.

'I thought that would make you laugh pet.'

Aunt Ede grew up in Wales and moved to England when she was just twenty-one, but still had a slight Welsh accent which could be heard sometimes.

'Come on Alora, let's go for a walk, you may see some familiar faces,' Alora seemed a bit dazed. 'Are you okay pet?' 'Yes, I was just thinking of Blake and how happy we were at the beginning and now this, but I am happy to see you Aunt Ede, no matter what.'

'Oh, don't dwell pet' Aunt Ede stood up and rubbed her hands before she took Alora's hand.

'Come on, come with me. We are all happy at the beginning love, it's the honeymoon period, it doesn't last, and life always throws obstacles in our way, but the honeymoon period, it's not real anyway, you don't even know one another properly, it's only when you start to spend time together and really get to know one and other that the relationship really starts, and those obstacles can be overcome when real love kicks in. Me and your Uncle Albert had our ups and downs love, but if it doesn't feel right in here,' she said as she put her hand to her heart, 'then you will know it too love.' I remember when you were only sixteen and you were sobbing over that boy, what was his name?…Johnny.'

Alora's face lit up, 'Aw Johnny, I don't know what happened to him, I heard he had moved back to Ireland, but then my dad told me he had died in an accident. I cried for weeks; he was here one minute then gone. Aw Johnny, she reflected in fondness, 'we did have a laugh, he was hilarious.'

Alora noted how Aunt Ede now walked freely without her walking stick, unlike before, especially towards the end of her life. Her hair was still in its old-fashioned style, but it was a lovely chestnut brown instead of a silver, grey colour. She was still wearing a flowery dress like she always had, a leafy green colour with white flowers on and the creamy warm smell of vanilla following her was still comforting. Her skin was always clear, however her face appeared to have less 'laughter lines' now as she called them. Her light blue eyes were sparkling, and her face still showed an amused expression with a hint of mischief in her smile. 'Are you happy here now that you have passed Aunt Ede?' Alora asked.

'Yes, my love,' she answered without hesitation while they walked through the never-ending room. Alora observed the people around her, there was a group of men to the right of her all of a similar age, playing cards and laughing, all dressed in like a military uniform. A young couple to the left of her that were dancing and also what looked like a whole family sitting around a cosy fireplace with what Alora assumed was their father reading a paper and their mother reading a children's story book to them all. A group of teenagers were in front of them playing basketball, everyone seemed to be enjoying themselves.

'How does it work here Aunt Ede? I mean all these people are they all just doing their thing?'

'Yes that's correct love, you can do what you like, go where you like, visit where you like, go back to a time on earth where you like at whatever age you may be, or you or you can go and observe what is going on back to your life on earth at present if you like, the choice is yours, where would you like to go?'

'Wow, I'm not sure, there is too much to choose from, I may go and see what ....'

'Is that.. is that **Johnny?**'

'**Alora** What's the story?'

'It is you Johnny oh wow, what are you doing here?'

'Haha' Johnny laughed, 'same as you I imagine, I take it you have just got here though, I have been here a while.'

'Why what happened?' Alora asked wide eyed.

'I crashed my bike when I was twenty-five well some eejit did, he drove into me and I went flying, broke nearly every bone in my body, I'm fine now though, what about you?'

'Well, I was in a car crash but...'

'She's not fully fledged yet Johnny' Aunt Ede interrupted.

'What do you mean Aunt Ede?' Alora quizzed.

'I mean you are here in spirit but back on earth you are

resting in a coma, so hence why no one can see you here, unless they knew you in a previous life like myself and Johnny.'

'Oh, I thought I had passed already.'

'No love not completely yet.'

'Ah best of both worlds Alora, you are looking great though, even though well, you know what I mean.'

'Thank you Johnny and you look ..older.' Alora said quietly, well I am I have been here eight years now I am the same age as you, thirty-three.'

'But I thought..' Alora said as she turned to Aunt Ede.

'I choose to be this age Alora I am in my mid-forties, I was ninety-two when I passed, but this is when I had most fun, so I chose this age.'

'Yeah and I'm going to stay at thirty-five I have decided so two more years and that's it, I won't age anymore.'

'Wow you really do get to choose in this life don't you?' Alora added positively.

'Yes you do plus, there is no pain, physically or mentally, no emotion, no illness, no problems we just have a ball don't we Ede?'

'For sure love, I was going to show Alora around, but if you fancy taking her somewhere then go for it.' Aunt Ede smiled and winked at Johnny; she could see there was some unfinished business between the two of them.

'Yes that would be nice, when are you free, tonight, tomorrow?' Alora asked Johnny innocently as he found himself laughing. 'Haha there is no time here, no tonight or tomorrow, it's just a constant, but on the plus side too, there is also no tiredness, no feeling of needing a rest, so therefore no sleep. I tell you what I will come and find you in a while, you go and have a wander with your aunt.' Johnny said as he pecked her on the cheek and then disappeared.

Alora continued to see a few of her family and friends that had passed previously, a couple of old school friends, but mainly elderly relatives, the rest of the millions of people around her, couldn't see her as she wasn't fully passed. They chose to visit Wales where Aunt Ede grew up and they sat by the stream in the sunshine and chatted close to the kids playing by the farmhouse, all unaware of Alora and Aunt Ede's presence. Alora decided to have a dip in the clear river waters, she loved to swim as a child and had not spared much time for it as an adult. She thought how strange it was to be able to swim and not get wet. They chatted about everything Aunt Ede had done since she had passed and all the places she had visited back to earth in spirit. Johnny suddenly appeared in the water next to a duckling that had caught Alora's eye from the side of the riverbank, dipping its head in the water and making tiny waves that move outwards from its drops. Aunt Ede decided to leave them to it for a while, they had a lot of catching up to do, she vanished into oblivion and Alora began to tell Johnny about her life and her relationship with Blake. She was aware of her arrival here and remembers her car being hit, however the time leading up to the crash was still a bit of a blur so they decided between the two of them they would work it out and Alora proceeded to tell Johnny her story.

He called her name; she didn't hear him over the noise of cars and taxi's hooting through the busy streets of London. He decided to run to catch up with her which made her jump.

'Sorry, he apologised as he noticed her beauty even more so than he had before glowing under the shimmer of the bright yellow streetlamp. The deafening music from the car that had stopped at the traffic lights now fading as it drove off as they both remain oblivious to the city street. She shuddered at his touch as he stroked her arm and moved closer. 'Not here,' she shuddered. He wrapped his suit jacket and wrapped it around her shoulders, and she felt the touch of his hand resting gently on her bottom over her silk fish tail dress.. Five-star hotels stood hugely on almost every street, and he guided her as she followed, submissively to the welcoming of the revolving door.

She knew it was wrong, he knew it was wrong, it didn't matter. Her whole body was longing for his touch like a powerful magnetic force.

The luxury of the honeymoon suite went unnoticed as he pushed her backwards onto the extra wide bed. He lowered himself on top of her, his mouth open as he lifted her dress, teasing her with his warm tongue on her neck while slowly removing her underwear. His tongue travelled slowly over her breasts down past her tummy while she removed his trousers. She let out a moan as her body trembled and her eyes opened and wandered to her empty bed. 'Wow, what a dream that was.'

Chapter Five

Alora

The beginning, five years earlier.

'So, you've got a date tonight then Lor?' Alora's house mate Cassy asks as she jumps in the passenger seat for her lift to work.

'Yep, third time this month, so, keep it quiet please Cass, just in case, you know.' Alora asks as she reflects to her last two disastrous dates.

'Yeah of course,' Cassy lies, with no conviction at all. Alora's last date was most probably up there in her top three, of disastrous dates for sure. She should have spotted the warning signs a mile off, she reflected in hindsight. Matt the rat, who had cancelled twice prior to them finally meeting was a definite no. As soon as he had introduced himself she had noticed the white untanned ring line on his wedding finger minus the ring. The constant vibration of missed calls on his phone, with his request to meet in the middle of nowhere, accompanied by his nervous, sweaty, agitated behaviour, which had also been a bit of a giveaway she reflected. She wasn't stupid, she had just been hopeful, excited, and very trusting. It was only when his wife came bolting in the restaurant accompanied by her sister, and the whack Matt took on the back of his head with his wife's handbag, yelling 'Me and the kids are going to take you for every penny you have, you are a cheating lying bastard,' did the penny finally drop. Dropped like a brick from a great height.

A few weeks later Alora decided to accept a date with Andrew at her local The Six bells.' Andrew seemed nice enough, he was a gentleman, he didn't drink, he didn't party, he also didn't like Alora's 'bold' clothes that she had been wearing that evening and had told her so, which didn't go down too well with Alora and neither did Andrew asking her to keep her voice down when she laughed out loud and ' too loud' according to Andrew, which was 'disrespectful to others,' also according to him. Safe to say their first day became their last.

'Third time lucky then Lor!' Cassy laughed as she tried to top up her lipstick in the passenger mirror just as Alora was going full on around the roundabout.

'Sorry Cass I missed the turning.'

Cassy worked at the preschool as a nursery teacher at Boadfield Primary school where Alora was teaching year six. Alora had been looking for a lodger for some extra funds and perhaps, some company, she didn't like living alone, one year on and Cassy was still there. It worked, eventually, after a little show down between the two where Alora had laid down some house rules. Even though Cassy and Alora couldn't be any more different.

Sadie

'Woosh two days until my 30th birthday party, that you are all trying to keep a secret, but it's so obvious ☺xx'

Sadie was the youngest, of her siblings and with three older brothers she was loved and spoilt rotten by their father, in her three older brother's opinion. She was convinced that there was a planned surprise party for her this weekend, *and* she was right. It was all being planned down to the most minor detail. She had been looking forward to her own 'surprise' party since she had turned twenty-nine.

Lucian

Lucian received a notification from his girlfriend, apologising for being a little off with him last night, he ignored it. He was getting fed up with her moods and the way she had been treating him lately.

'Don't forget Sadie's party Friday night, love you. Xx'
He had never even met Sadie, and all he ever heard from his girlfriend Lisa was what a 'princess' Sadie was. *'Women.'*

Lucian was a good-looking man, with piercing blue eyes and dark hair, he also had the most gorgeous smile, unbeknown to him. He was a remarkably successful businessman and at thirty-two, he now had his own company with eight employees and his car hire and sales business was growing fast.

'If only he was as successful in choosing his women,'

his mate Jez had advised him once. He did go for a certain type. A high maintenance type.

Cassy

Cassy and Alora waited patiently for the automatic doors to open at 7.45am. Alora's classed started at 8.50am, Cassy's 8.00am. Alora loved to arrive early and prepare and organise her day. Cassy was just grateful for the lift and to arrive on time. Two minutes later the buzzer rang, Cassy turned back to open the door to the school's new teacher, Kyle Bailey.

'He's hot.' Cassy mouthed to Alora as she rushed off to the preschool club leaving Alora's rolling eyes behind.

Kyle

Kyle (Mr. Bailey) as he would be known by the end of the day had an excellent report as a teacher. His decision to leave Waverly Secondary school had not been an easy one and he was reminded of this as he drove past on his way to his new post at Boadfield Primary this morning. As he followed Alora's lead he had a sudden realisation of how much he loved teaching and how he had missed it. His colleagues seemed nice enough, and there were a couple of lovely looking teachers similar to his own age, especially Alora, he thought. He snapped himself out of his thoughts, he didn't want any romance to ruin his career. Again.

Blake

Blake had finished work on time and as he popped his new shades on, the mid May sun was beating down onto his face as he eagerly pulled on to the short dual carriageway drive to his home.

Within an hour he was showered and had opened a new bottle of aftershave, an unopened Christmas present. His crisp ironed mint green shirt brought out his dark brown eye colour and his blonde hair was behaving himself due to its new hair cut he managed to fit in on Saturday in the high street, just before closing.

His first date in ten years. He reflected glumly for a moment to where he was this time last year, newly divorced, missing his two kids and crashing on his best mate Russ's sofa, drinking too much, eating too much, and gambling all his earnings. Within a year he had turned his life around after he had hit his own rock bottom. He had sought help for his gambling and started a new business running a car repair shop. He had also found himself a nice three bedroomed apartment for himself and his children, who would stay with him at alternative weekends. His ex-wife Ann could still give him grief for no reason; however, he had grown up and he had a healthy relationship with their two children, and if they were happy, then so was he.

'That'll do.' He told himself as his phone beeped.

'Sadie's surprise party Fri night, bring your new date if u want m8.'

Blake had met Sadie at primary school, through Russ

his friend. Sadie was Russ's sister, she had been his first crush, yet she had broken his heart when she had finished with him for Ryan Crane when he was twelve, after becoming his girlfriend for just one day, well 23 hours and 10 minutes Blake had counted. Russ had never let him forget; he did finally get over his crush on his best friend's sister when he had married Ann, his now ex-wife. Blake had bumped into Sadie on a night out in town and had told him she would always love him and left a red lipstick pattern on his cheek. He had questioned her words; *'did she actually love him? Was it a drunken chat? Or did she love him as a brother?'* It was hard to tell with Sadie, she flirted with everyone.

Alora's taxi had arrived, she checked herself in the antique oak based oval mirror in the hall and fiddled with her golden blonde ceramic curls and then quickly wiped off a layer of her peach-coloured tinted lip gloss. *'Too much, that's better.'* 'I'm off now Cass, see you later.' Cass flung out of the living room door to the hall and looked Alora up and down.

'Wow you look lush, go for it girl.' She said opened mouth. Alora thanked her awkwardly.

Cassy was open about her bisexuality, it didn't matter to Alora apart from when Cassy looked her up and down in that 'Cassy way,' like she just had, and also another time when a drunken Cassy had tried to kiss her on the lips. Alora had told her firmly that she wasn't interested.

The taxi ride was a short journey that had taken Alora to a central pub in the West End, called 'The Optimist,' arriving early as usual, Alora was rarely late and when she walked in she recognised the blonde-haired man at the bar with a mint green nicely ironed shirt at once from his picture on the dating app. She walked towards him nervously until she was standing equally to his left.

'Alora?' Blake asked holding out his hand.

'Yes, hi, Blake?' She giggled.

'Nice to meet you.' Blake smiled brightly as he gave Alora a very firm handshake in an almost businesslike manner Alora noted, his hands were very warm, and she wondered if he was as nervous as she was.

'Would you like a drink?'

'Yes please, disaronno and coke please, no ice thanks.'

Kyle

The first-person Kyle noticed was Alora as he popped into 'The Optimist' for a quick drink after his first day of teaching as she was heading from the ladies past the bar.

'Well, hi again,' he smiled more excitedly than he had intended to, revealing a cute dimple in his chin.

'Hello, er Kyle, again haha,' Alora giggled as her eyes travelled onto the cute dimple.

'Drink?' Kyle asked as he pushed his thick dark curls away from his face.

'No, I'm with, thank you, I mean, I am on a date with, Blake.' She pointed over to the table in the corner with an already observant Blake holding up his hand as if to say, *'Sorry bud, she's with me.'*

'No problem, enjoy your evening.' Kyle said happily

as he smiled at Alora and gave Blake a quick nod.

'That's weird, that was Kyle, the new teacher at the school I work at, he started today.' Alora felt like she had to justify.

'Oh right, yes you were saying you teach, what age?'

Alora started to tell Blake all about her working life until she asked the obligatory 'less about me, what about you?'

As the evening went on Alora and Blake found themselves comfortable in each other's company, he was attractive Alora thought, in a kind of 'Viking looking kind of way and appeared to have a cool but calm approach too, as she described him to Cassy, who was waiting with anticipation to hear everything about him. 'A true gentleman too.' Alora said smiling.

'I can't believe you bumped into the new teacher, Kyle, now he *is* hot, bet he is no gentleman.' Cassy laughed. Unlike Alora, who was looking to settle down and have children, Cassy wasn't interested in domestic bliss just yet. She was happy to 'just have a bit of fun' and at twenty-six years old, just a few years younger than Alora she enjoyed her no strings attached sex, male or female.

Blake felt like the date had gone well, he was hoping it had for Alora too, he thought she was very pretty and quite funny too and appeared to know her own mind. He assumed that she must be fond of children being a schoolteacher, which was a good thing as he already had two of his own, which gave him the confidence to invite her to his friend's sister's surprise 30th birthday party on Friday night.

Sadie's 30th 'surprise birthday party

Sadie pursed her cherry red lips and admired her reflection in her dressing table mirror. Her newly styled long raven hair, curled nicely below her shoulders. Her sun kissed tan glowing through her perfectly applied professional make up. Her little black dress that she had treated herself to cost 'more than a month's wage,' criticised her brother Tim, who was also her accountant.

'Thirrrrty how did that happen?' Sadie mouthed the word thirty slowly to herself in the mirror. *'Still living at home with my parents and still single however, I run a successful beauty business and I look twenty-five if that,'* She convinced herself.

'The two taxis arrived at Sadie's parents and waited patiently as Sadie popped her jimmy choo shoes on. She sat excitedly in the back of the taxi while taking a few selfies with the caption 'fit at 30' ready to upload onto her Instagram account. Within a few minutes the taxi had pulled up to the secluded, beautiful grounds of the only 5-star hotel in the area. The last time she had been here was on a spa day with her employee's checking out the competition whilst enjoying being pampered. She acted totally surprised upon entry to the beautifully decorated darkened room with pink fairy lights reflecting on a beautifully created balloon arch spelling 'Happy 30th Sadie' to the sound of Stevie Wonder's Happy Birthday song. As the lights came on, over two hundred guests welcomed her with party poppers and recordings and pictures of her from their mobile phones of her entry. Her friend and employee Lisa stood directly in front of her in a short peach dress, she was the first-person Sadie recognised. On Lisa's right there was at least five people that Sadie hadn't met before, although one man caught her attention, he was standing to the right of Lisa, leaning casually on a post dressed in a very smart but casual combination and he caught Sadie's eye instantly as the most handsome man she had ever seen in her life. Lucian.

'Wow, he is gorgeous, how could she be cheating on that!' Sadie thought disgustedly as they were introduced. Sadie liked to keep her relationship with her staff completely professional, when it suited her, and would naturally sometimes overhear conversations, and on the odd occasion, on a team night out and after a few drinks, her staff would talk and reveal personal aspects of their lives. Sadie was a good listener, in fact, Sadie, loved to listen, she was exceptionally good at revealing very little about herself but at the same time finding out all she could about her staff. Sadie had also overheard Lisa telling her receptionist that she had been receiving messages from her ex and had arranged to secretly meet him. Sadie would use this information to her advantage, unfortunately for Lisa, and by the end of the evening Lisa had stormed out of the party leaving Lucian open to Sadie's clutches.

'Happy 30th to me.' Sadie smiled.

'Jeez she doesn't waste any time this Sadie one does she.. then again neither did this Lucian fella.' commented Johnny.

The affair

Her

Her phone said 2.17am and she felt pathetic. She was acting like a love-struck teenager over a silly text and a silly kiss. She had the bed to herself as her partner had crashed out on the sofa. She wasn't bothered at all. She stared again at her message. 'You look gorgeous tonight.' A stark contrast to her partners 'You'll do' earlier as she mentally returned the compliment back and had noted how good he looked tonight too. She hadn't really noticed it before or looked at him in that way. Ever.

The thought of her friend entered her mind, she pushed that thought back and replaced it with a moment from earlier in the evening, where she caught site of his eyes all over her body in her little black dress. He had noticed her, complimented her, and paid her some attention. Why? Her head told her to do the right thing and tell her friend what had happened and do the honourable thing like she normally would and take her own advice that she would gladly preach to all, but her heart was secretly enjoying the much-needed attention as she wasn't receiving any at home. In fact, things hadn't been great at home for a while.

She wondered about him, 'was he awake? Was he thinking of her? Was he sleeping alone? Should she reply to his compliment?' She started to type and then decided not to send it, but then changed her mind again.

Him

He was looking forward to a little interrogation when they got home tonight. He thought that maybe in her drunken state she would let slip her secret little gathering in the car with another man, no chance of that now as she lay fully clothed minus her shoes on the sofa, she didn't even make it upstairs to the bedroom. He popped a quilt over her and put a glass of fresh water on the coffee table and went to bed.

By the early hours, his only companion was his bedroom television, until his phone started vibrating on his bedside table.

'Was this text meant for me?'

He stared at his phone for a moment and then started to type.

'Hey, yes it was for you. I thought you looked gorgeous, and I wanted to tell you as I hadn't noticed you before until that night I kissed you. I kissed you and you responded because let's face it none of us are getting any attention at home and now I have heard that my woman was seen in a car up close and personal with another man.

Look I love her but I would have sex with you if you wanted to especially if she is playing away and if I'm honest thinking about you now in that little black dress is turning me on and if you was here now in my bed while she was asleep downstairs, I would happily take you to bed.' He didn't send it. He ignored the silly question put his phone down and let his imagination run wild instead.

Chapter Six

'So, you are a schoolteacher now then Lor get you, what do you teach?'

'Have a guess Johnny?'

'Cooking?'

'Get lost, I know you are taking the p...'

'What was it you burnt, and you had to throw that saucepan away and we had to buy a new one before your dad got home?'

'Boiled eggs Johnny.' Alora replied with a laugh.

'Ha ha that's right Lor, how would you like your eggs.. hahah.''

'P off I was fourteen.'

'And I distracted you I know, and P off, you still say that? I remember you would never swear, well ya know every other word is a swear word back in Ireland haha, anyway joking aside what do you teach?'

'I said guess Johnny.'

'English.'

'Nope.'

'History.'

'No guess again.'

'P.E? you were always good at sport.'

'No, …. geography.'

'Really? Brilliant, good on you Lor,.. have you made the children a magic map yet?'

'Oh my god I had forgotten all about the magic map! I loved it.'

'I know it was great…'

'Took me ages to design that.'

'It was highly creative Lor, and we could go wherever we wanted to, it's a bit like now really, we can go anywhere you would like to go, pick a place and we could be there in a flash.'

'Okay erm let me think…. I know Bray! The Gateway to the Garden of Ireland.'

'You remembered!' Johnny was impressed.

'Of course, I do, you used to visit there when we were kids and you never stopped banging on about it, and you promised to take me there one day!'

'And I promised you I would keep my promise, come on follow me.' Johnny stretched his arms out in a flying motion and as daft as it would have seemed to Alora previously, here it was most natural thing to do.

'We are flying Johnny! Woah I love it.'

'We are free like the birds; look to your left can you see the emerald Isle?' Johnny pointed.

'Wow is that Ireland?'

'Yes we are here now Lor.'

'That was quick Johnny.'

'Yep quicker than the Dublin bus for sure, that was some long arse ride when we were kids.' Johnny recalled, 'only cos you weren't with me though.'

'Aw Johnny, it is really good to see you again.' Alora replied with a smile as herself and Johnny landed themselves onto a cliff looking out onto an array of infinite blue.

'Beautiful eh Lor?'

'Aw yes it is and that hue of gold shining below us, its magical.'

'It's the sand.' Johnny beamed.

'Ha I know Johnny, but I have never sat on a cliff and looked down before, do you not remember my fear of heights back home?'

'I do, I remember you telling me about that school trip to Paris and you were the only one that didn't go up to the top of the Eiffel Tower, what a waste Lor.'

'I know I didn't tell my mum and dad because they had bought me a nice new camera and wondered why I hadn't taken any photos from there, I told them that I had left my camera on the coach haha, but I'm not scared now look Johnny..' Alora proudly showed off a perfect cartwheel.

'You are still as agile as ever, and what is there to be scared of, as I always say you cannot worry about things that haven't happened yet sweetheart, the fear of the unknown can be a bastard if you let it, so don't. The excitement of the unknown is so much better trust me; you cannot worry about things that you cannot change and some things you can't Lor.'

'You are so right, and I don't feel scared or worried or anything here with you, even though I am here because I was in a car accident, but my life was a mess, well my relationship with Blake was.'

'Well I'm all ears, so tell me all about it and how do you fancy walking and talking, I have never completed this whole walk before it's 6km from here in Bray to Greystones and if you fall it doesn't matter because I will catch you and if I fall you can catch me and, if we both fall we can land on our feet, in fact watch this!' Johnny had leaped off the cliff before Alora could blink, and she found herself looking down at him waving at her from the shore. 'Haha you mad head you.'

'See how easy that was, Johnny said proudly as he landed back on top of the cliff withing seconds, his green eyes smiling into Alora's.

Alora stood there mesmerized for a moment as she recalled the first time she had looked into Johnny's eyes back to when she was only fourteen, she recalled how Johnny eyes were the kind of green that would always look bright and soft at the same time, yet they would speak to her soul with no words needed. She always felt safe when Johnny looked into her eyes and there was a familiarity between them that had given her comfort too.

The whisper of the sea accompanying them both as they chatted freely along the cliff walk, the suns rays illuminating as if to create a path for their steps for just the two of them and their eyes only, as Alora continued with her story.

The affair

Her

She checked her phone as soon as she awoke. No, nothing no reply. She felt silly, pathetic even, and deleted her message that she had sent to him. She started to delete the message she had received from him too, 'You look gorgeous tonight.' She paused for a moment and then screen shotted the message before deleting it and changed his name in her contacts to 'Lily.'

She decided to make a real effort with her appearance today, she had also recently bought some expensive perfume for herself. She wants his attention, and she is going to get it, one way or another by teasing him at work, especially with the lack of attention at home, plus she couldn't remember the last time she had received perfume as a gift.

Her short dress is fitting and creaseless, her stilettoes high and her hair immaculately behaving itself she notices as she admires her own reflection. Her stomach cartwheels as soon as she sees his face, which is poker straight, almost businesslike, although she catches his eyes looking at her from behind as she walks in front of him with a slight wiggle that she has added to her walk. She turns around and scans his eyes, they cannot lie, they cannot remain professional as hard as he tries. She smiles to herself as she enjoys the tease, and tells herself to enjoy the game, if that's what it is, if he wants to play then she will have some fun with him.

Him

He smiled to himself as he noticed how hot she looked today. He knew it was for him. He pretended not to notice; it was all part of the fun. She was a distraction for him, an escapism from his thoughts of his partner at home, who was becoming more distant. The thought of his partner playing away had been haunting him as he lay awake all last night as he watched her sleep. He loved her deeply, however he couldn't confront her, not now, not after he had kissed her friend, what right did he have? The truth will come out in the end, he knew that, and that's why he needed to remain professional, especially at work, there were eyes and ears everywhere.

He would keep his options open he decided as he watched her wiggle in front of him. She smelt good today too, but he didn't trust her completely and he needed to keep her on side. He regretted sending her that text telling her she looked gorgeous, hopefully she had deleted it as she had a partner too, so hopefully she was being discreet. That dress, it really did compliment her figure, if she carries on looking that hot he may have to take it off for her. Not today though, he was tired, he was busy, however she had brightened up a very dull morning.

Chapter Seven

Sadie felt the emptiness to the side of her in her bed. She had awoken with a mixture of feeling smug and a little guilty after her 30th birthday party where she had caused a big argument between her employee Lisa and the lovely Lucian. She had tried to persuade Lucian, to join her for a night cap, he had declined, gracefully.

Her head hurt, her mouth was dry, but the picture in her mind about the way the lovely Lucian had looked at her last night, put a smile on her face. She reached for her phone, it had 4% charge, so she fumbled for her power bank in her Gucci handbag and stumbled to the shower, using the complimentary hair and shower gel and sighed at the thought of the only hair conditioner she used was at home sitting nicely in her ensuite cabinet. She wrapped herself in a towel and checked all of her notifications and messages. Nothing from Lucian. She was sure she had put her number in his phone. She tried searching him on face book and all of her social media, although with no surname she found nothing. A ping on her phone gave her a second of hope until she realised it was a text message from Lisa, her employee Lucian's now ex-girlfriend.

'I hope you are happy now you nasty bitch!'

Lucian was trying his best to ignore the constant vibrations and buzzing from his phone. Lisa had been ringing him all morning. He couldn't be bothered with her screaming, which she had been doing a lot of lately. In his mind they had been coming to an end for a while and last night had confirmed it. She had also been sneaking around with her phone lately while at his house. She had also become a little bit too neurotic for him too. It hadn't helped when recently some cash had gone missing from the house, plus, she was always talking about her ex-Chris, yet she wanted to know Lucian's every move and Lucian had felt suffocated. They had dated for a year, and it was currently going nowhere. He had treated her fine as far as he was concerned, he had taken her to some nice places, helped her out financially when she had needed it. He hadn't even flirted with another woman, let alone anything else. Until last night. *'Lisa's boss too. Shit.'*. He did like her though, Sadie, it had been a last-minute decision to attend her party, under duress, he hadn't planned for the night to end the way it had. Sadie had intrigued him though, there was just something about her, she was stunning to look at, he remembered her eyes, her big brown eyes, her raven hair and a vulnerability which he found quite endearing.

They had talked for a while, well he had listened, she had done most of the talking. She had left her number in his phone, but for now he would switch it off for some peace and quiet.

Lisa was fuming. *'I know what you done last night and if you think I am working for you EVER again then you must be joking! Oh, and btw I have messaged all of your regulars and told them that you sometimes use the cheap cream for their facials and pretend to use the expensive one!! Plus, a lot of them will be coming to me now at my house and if you try and do anything about it I will ruin your business. Good luck with Lucian the womaniser, you two are suited. Slag!!* **Sadie Sent**.

'Well, you didn't waste any time did you, you are welcome to Princess Sadie, it won't last you are both as bad as each other! **Lucian Sent.**

Blake reached for his phone for one thing only, to see if Alora had replied, she hadn't just yet. He reflected on last night at Sadie's surprise party, he had enjoyed himself and it appeared Alora had too, even if she had been a little unsteady on her feet towards the end of the evening he had noted. She had been showing off her moves on the dance floor with Blake, Russ, Sadie and what looked like, towards then end of the evening Sadie's new man Lucian, he was sure that is what Alora said his name was he recalled, 'handsome Lucian,' to be exact were her words. Blake had accompanied Alora home in a taxi like a true gent and sent her a goodnight text when he was home. She still hadn't replied, that was at 1.12am this morning. It was now 11.45am and a beautiful Saturday it was. He slipped his phone in his pocket after checking his messages one last time then headed off to his local, 'The Bull' to watch the football.

Alora could not believe the time, she hadn't slept in for this long in ages. She had drunk quite a lot of alcohol last night, the pain in her head was reminding her of it now, although she hadn't forgotten Cassy her flat mate halfway up the stairs in a compromising position with Kyle, AKA Mr. Bailey, the new teacher. Cassy was incredibly open about her sexual adventures Alora thought as she reached for the bottle of fizzy water on her bedside table, *'but Mr. Bailey, already! They had only met a few days ago!'* Alora would never let a man near her so early, she judged as she reached for her phone and noticed it was out of charge. There was a knock on her bedroom door which was then followed by Cassy walking straight in, but with a nice strong cup of coffee accompanied by a hint of *'Sorry I was having sex on your stairs and it is your house'* unwritten, unspoken apology, *'but I have made you a strong coffee just as you like it, so don't lecture me'* tone. Then she proceeded to tell Alora all about her evening prior to the sex on the stairs event.

Cassy had popped to the Six bells just an hour before last orders after her night in on her own had become 'too boring' and upon entry she had noticed Kyle sitting at a table near the entrance with a woman who was clearly upset. He had asked Cassy where Alora was at first.

'He clearly fancies you Alora, 'Cassy stated in a 'but I'm not bothered' kind of way, 'it was only when I told him that we lived together he was happy to come back here. At first, when I saw him consoling this woman I assumed it was his girlfriend, but he then introduced her to me as his sister, Lisa, who had just split up with her boyfriend Lucian or something at some surprise birthday party and …'

Alora put two and two together, she worked out that Kyle's sister Lisa *had* been the one at the party who had had a massive row with the good-looking Lucian, and she had left the party early in distress. This Lucian, and Sadie whose party it was, *had* been remarkably close with each other towards the end of the evening. She didn't remember much after that, apart from travelling home in a taxi with Blake before discovering Cassy and Kyle on her stairs. In her state of her hangover, she simply couldn't be bothered to say anything.

Kyle was listening to Lisa on loudspeaker as he answered his phone and rubbed a towel through his hair and proceeded to get dressed. She had been telling him all about her revenge social media activities. Kyle rolled his eyes. She didn't do things by half did his sister Lisa, there was always a drama with her, he had been there for her last night when she had called him in hysterics and asked him to pay the taxi from some lavish hotel halfway out of town and to meet him in the 'Six bells.' He had been planning on an early night, but she had no one else, no family anyway, they only really had each other, here in London. Their mother had died a few years earlier and they never knew their father. Their only family were cousins, aunts and one grandma back in Ireland. After consoling Lisa, he had bumped into Cassy and the next thing he knew he was around her house and as he was going up the stairs, she threw herself at him until the lovely Alora had arrived home.

By the end of the sunny weekend, Blake had received a reply from Alora, and they had arranged a third date, which pleased him immensely. Cassy and Kyle had both agreed via text, that they would remain professional at work, which was not too hard as they worked in different departments.

Lucian had finally messaged Sadie on Sunday afternoon and Sadie was secretly pleased, she was slightly annoyed that it had taken him so long to contact her, she wasn't used to waiting and they arranged a date for midweek.

Lisa had told Kyle that she had spent the weekend taking as many clients off Sadie as she could, and that she would eventually open up a beauty parlour that would be even more successful than 'Sadie's.' Also, she had blocked Lucian from all of her social media but decided to 'keep' Sadie's contact unblocked so that she could see what 'they' were up to, but she would never forget what Sadie and Lucian had done to her. Kyle advised her that this Lucian guy was just as guilty as Sadie and that she was definitely better off without the pair of them.

Two months on, Lucian and Sadie, Blake and Alora, Kyle and Cassy were all officially dating, and Cassy had decided to look for another job. What she did not realise after she had uploaded her CV and applied for the exiting new role that her knew boss that she was yet to meet would turn out to be Lucian.

'So, are you free next Saturday Kyle?' Cassy asked Kyle as she was checking her platinum white bobbed hair in his bathroom mirror.

'Yeah think so, why what you have got planned?'

'Lucian and his girlfriend Sadie have invited us to his house for a dinner party. Cassy confirmed to a non-responding Kyle.

'Did you hear me? My boss Lucian has…..'

'Lucian? Yeah should be okay, what time?'

'Seven pm.'

'Okay yeah fine.'

Cassy had made herself quite at home at Kyle's house. She liked her own space as did Kyle and in Cassy's words she 'didn't do love,' she just wanted some fun, which suited Kyle too.

Cassy jumped on the bed and snatched the tv remote from Kyle and switched off the television and started to tickle his chest and instantly Kyle let out a huge sigh.

'Look I'm just tired, we had a heavy night and it's your fault you wore me out so …' Kyle justified.

'Yeah well, I get the hint, anyway I have had a message from my brother's girlfriend Chloe, and she wants me to go clothes shopping with her.'

'You go shopping, I just need to chill, I may have a sleep later and if you fancy it we can do something to night, a meal, cinema or whatever.'

'Yeah okay.' Kyle liked Cassy she was fun and full of life, sometimes a little too wild for Kyle if the truth be known. She had petite pixie like features, with a platinum blonde sharp bobbed haircut. Big blue eyes that she used sometimes to get her own way, and the longest shapeliest legs he had ever seen. The main attraction for Kyle was that she was caring. She had shown this when she had consoled his sister Lisa after she had been dumped by some rat that he was never introduced to, called Lucian.

'Oh, hang on a minute...Lucian and his girlfriend Sadie, could it be the same Lucian that dumped Lisa, his sister?'

The Dinner Party

Sadie was running around straightening the flowers in the hanging basket in the conservatory where the pre meal nibbles and drinks would take place. She had moved into Lucian's new build that he had not long purchased, just over a year ago.

'The flowers are fine Sadie could you just set the table please?' Lucian asked as he started to prepare the spiced carrot and lentil soup. He was just the best cook ever as Sadie had told her staff, although she wasn't just with him for his culinary skills either she had joked previously.

'Okay will do, just trying to make it look pretty, so how many have you got coming in total again?'

'Well, I have invited my mate Jez and his misses Sarah and them two next door, Sophie and Tim, you met them last week didn't you as we were pulling out on the drive, and Cassy from work and her fella Kyle, your mate Blake and his new girlfriend, whatever her name is....Alora, so yeah there will be ten of us.'

'Ding dong.'

'Oh, someone's early, I'll get it.' Sadie raced through to the front door pumping up one of the floral cushions on her way that she had purchased to give Lucian's home 'a woman's touch.'

'Hello, hiya.'

'Sorry if we are a little early but living next door I thought we may as well get to know one another, and I can give you a hand if you need me to?' Sophie the dark-haired petite woman suggested as Sadie blew her and her husband Tim an air kiss and thanked them for the bottle of Red Vin Sweet.

'Thank you, but we have everything under control, but we can start on this.' Sadie giggled.

Tim strolled through to Lucian in the kitchen and made small talk while the two ladies got to know one another over their glass of red.

'So how long have you and Tim been together?'

'Oh, five years and Tim proposed on our anniversary last week.' Sophie said while she excitedly flashed her left hand to show off her gold ring with its Ruby stone. Her hands were tiny and so was the stone Sadie observed. 'Congratulations, oh we should open the champagne after this, any excuse haha.'

'Thank you, what about you and Lucian how long have you been together?' Sadie hesitated for a moment.

'Oh, not long, you know but it feels longer, in an enjoyable way of course.' Sadie answered as she stared at Sophie's eyebrows thinking that they could do with a tint and a tidy, she could not help herself sometimes, she was a beautician after all, and she noticed these things. Sophie was naturally pretty, with dark brown coloured hair, which was swept back in an Alice band, showing off her unkept eyebrows. Sophie wore no make-up and had no tan, there was no need for it with her olive complexion, unlike Sadie who topped up her 'self-tan 'at work every week, she envied for a moment.

As the two women became acquainted Sophie did wonder what had happened to Lisa, Lucian's ex, they had met once briefly when Lucian was moving in, however her thoughts were interrupted by the doorbell as she wandered to the kitchen with her champagne to Tim and Lucian'

'Hey Blake!' Sadie threw her arms around him and gave him an almighty squeeze while planting a firm red lipstick mark on his left cheek.

'Hey Sadie, how are you?' Blake asked with his face a little flushed while rubbing his cheek. 'You have met Alora haven't you before at your birthday, but I will re-introduce, Alora Sadie, Sadie, Alora.'

'Yes I remember you Alora a little worse for wear if I recall.' Sadie giggled. Alora smiled while thinking *'and you weren't!'* 'Yes I was by the time I was introduced to you but not enough to forget the evening.' Alora replied quickly, without directly saying it, but insinuating that she, like most of the party goers knew exactly what had happened and how Sadie had met Lucian that night at her 30th birthday by him dumping his ex on the dance floor.

'Come through guys.' Sadie welcomed totally ignoring Alora's comment but instantly noticing her dark roots coming through to her golden blonde locks. Another potential client for the salon Sadie thought as she had recently added a hairdressers to the beauty salon.

'Ding dong.'

Two couples stood on the doorstep, Sadie had no idea who they were, she knew Lucian's mate Jez was coming with his partner and one of Lucian's employees Cassy and her partner.

'Hello, er you must be..'

'You must be Sadie.' Jez gave a firm and formal handshake; this is my wife Sarah.' Jez gave a hint of a New Zealand accent and had the build of a rugby player and played the sport very well. His wife Sarah was of a similar height with a similar accent and gorgeous dark skin with a mass of natural curls.

'Please to meet you both.' Sadie welcomed with her automatic handshake response.

'I am Cassy, this is Kyle.' Cassy introduced stepping forward brazenly and full of confidence. *'Wow, could her skirt be any shorter!'* Sadie noted as she welcomed the confident, platinum blonde wide eyed slim lady with legs to die for into the house. Her partner Kyle was a good looker as well, quite similar to Lucian she noted, almost identical in height and build. Sadie took them all through to the kitchen and accepted the bottles of prosecco and white wine. The soup was simmering on the low and the main course was confirmed by Lucian's, 'hello folks, none of you are vegan or vegetarian are you, but just in case …' he paused for a moment as Kyle approached him.

'So, you must be Cassy's partner Kyle.' Lucian stretched out his hand.

'And you must be Lucian.'

The sudden silence was deafening for a few seconds before Kyle took one swipe with his right fist and knocked Lucian flying. 'And that is from my sister Lisa!' **Smack!**

Menu

Starter

Spiced carrot and lentil soup

Main

Beef tagliata with rocket and parmigiano reggiano

Dessert

Cream Brulee / Home baked profiteroles

Three courses ruined.

Chapter Eight

'Woah jeez what an introduction, so what happened did your man hit him back?' Johnny asked laughing.

'Oh Johnny it wasn't funny at the time trust me, and no Kyle just walked straight out after he said, 'that was from my sister Lisa,' we all just stood there in a state of shock to be honest, including Lucian, it took a while for everyone to realise that Kyle was *the* Lisa's brother, the same Lisa who had been seeing Lucian.'

'Lisa the one he dumped for this Sadie one?'

'Correct, he's actually a nice man though Kyle, I know I work with him and.. well, he has been good to me, plus he explained that there were things that Lisa had done that had become apparent after. He admitted to me that he had always been a bit overprotective over his sister, especially since their mum had died when he was only young, and I don't think they ever knew their dad. It was awkward for us all at first, especially introducing her boyfriend to her new boss and he smacks him on introduction. Sadie wanted Lucian to ring the police and to fire Cassy and then obviously when Kyle had calmed down he was worried about his job, being a teacher. Word had got around; I think from one of Lucian's neighbours and …'

'Oh look, hello mister,' Johnny was distracted by a bird with dark feathers that had placed itself on the cliff side they were approaching, 'It's a cormorant Lor and it's letting us get closer and closer,' Johnny whispered, 'and I don't know why I am whispering because I don't think he can hear or see us.'

'Oh, right it's got quite a long thin bill hasn't it?'

'Yes and its wingspan can go up to about thirty-nine inches, but I have never been this close, here little fella.'

'It makes sense that he hasn't flown away yet, if that's the case we could get really close, are there any seals here? I love seals but back in England when I try and get close to them in the sea they swim away.' Alora sighed.

'Of course, they have been spotted here, but there was case where a seal pup was spotted on shore alone after a storm and the Gardai warned the public to stay away from it, because if it's mum smells any human scent on it she may abandon it and it can then take up to three weeks to shed its white fur before it takes to the sea and joins its mum.'

'Aw how sweet did it join its mum?'

'Yes Lor apparently it did, 'oh he is off, going down to the shore to catch its prey now,'

'Maybe it can sense us Johnny you never know.'

'Well, we are as free as that bird ya know, anywhere where was we what happened?'

'Yes, well eventually Kyle apologised to Lucian and Kyle kept his job, as did Cassy, and we all ended up in the same circle of friends. The lads would watch footie together and us girls would do yoga together and cinema.'

'And the pub of course?' Johnny assumed.

'Well not for me after a while, I will tell you about that later. Anyway, as I was saying one year on and dinner party number two...' 'No pub? What's wrong with ya?' Johnny laughed, 'hey, do you remember that fight I had with Aaron Hughes, over you?'

'How could I forget; his mum was best friends with my mum until they moved away. In fact, I haven't seen him in years, have you ...'

'No, before you ask that I haven't seen him here either, I guess he must be alive and kicking somewhere, annoying some poor fucker.'

'Well yeah he was a bit of an idiot really and a bully, but we were only kids, maybe he is a really nice person now and has a wife and kids.' Alora said innocently.

'That's what I love about you always hoping for the best, always seeing the good in everyone and it's quite endearing to see you haven't changed a bit. We had some fun didn't we girl.'

'Yes we did, until you broke my heart, although I didn't know for sure that you had passed.'

'Did I really?' Johnny laughed.

'Its not funny, I was inconsolable for months!'

'Really, aw bless your young heart, you do know your dad told me to steer clear of you don't ya?'

'No!' When?'

'When he caught us together, the day after I sneaked into yours, he came round my house, my ma and da was out, he threatened me, I wasn't scared of much but your da well I was frightened a bit of him, we all were on the estate, all the lads, he had a temper.'

'He sure did.'

'Did? as he passed? If he has I haven't seen him.'

'No, he hasn't but he has a slow start of dementia.'

'Bless him, what about your ma?'

'Yes, she's good thanks still keeping herself busy.'

'Sweet that is, how about your brother Joe?'

'Yes he's good thanks, married and has two kids one of each, twins actually Bethany and Brody they will be four soon.' Alora beamed.

'I take it you don't have any, which surprises me you used to say you wanted four by the time you were twenty-eight, you crazy sod ya.'

'Is that why you run away back to Ireland?'

'Haha still got ya sense of humour then, and no, of course not I would have loved kids, you know me coming from a big Irish family, no dad got ill, he passed and then ma didn't really settle in England. I worked for months to save for me first bike and bang, here I am. I look down on me ma and the others some days and she is still busy as always, looking after my nieces and nephews a lot now. Grandma is still alive bless her, she's getting on now, but I will take you if you want, to my ma's. I can show you me granny, me nieces and nephews and where I used to hang out, we will do a road trip,'

'The irony.' They both laughed.

The Driver

As the light spread across the inside of my eyelids I awoke to the realisation of this nightmare. I had dreamt incessantly last night, mainly about Alora, she had agreed to meet me at the funfair, I had no idea where this funfair was, but I walked around for what seemed like hours trying to find her. I suppose in the reality of the dream it was only seconds. I never found her. God this is awful, I rarely say a prayer, but I am desperate. I need to check on Alora, I need to know how she is, its driving me crazy. We have so many fond memories and I need to remind her of those, if she is okay of course and if she can hear me and only then I will confess to being the driver that hit her. If I go to the police then I won't get to see her at all. I don't care if they throw away the key, I just need to explain my reasons to Alora first.

Pretending is not easy for me, neither is keeping a low profile and now it has become exponentially harder after what has happened, my feelings for Alora have only become deeper.

My mind is made up I am going to see her.

To love maybe risky.
Not to love is foolish.

Chapter Nine

Present

The morning after the accident

3.17am and Lucian was struggling to sleep. He struggled to sleep through the night on his sofa in normal situations, however he did not want to be anywhere near Sadie after what she had done, plus, her telling the police that he and Alora had been more than just friends. Sadie had pushed him to the limit. He hadn't meant to say what he said last night, but Sadie had pushed and pushed until he had finally snapped.

'At a time like this as well when Alora is fighting for her life Sadie, and why would you tell the police about that nonsense about me and her?'

'Sorry, I just didn't think, I am concerned for Alora of course I am, but you have guilt written all over your face Lucian. Just like you did when I walked in on you and her cuddling that time.'

'I was consoling her; she had been crying for god's sake woman. Really Sadie you are something else, I thought you would have learnt by now, especially after what has recently just happened.'

'Well perhaps that's what you were planning on doing

all along, leaving me for her, maybe it's not Mia that you want, it's Alora.'

'Maybe I was, maybe I'm in love with her or maybe she would treat me better than you do cos she hasn't got a vile mouth like you have and neither has Mia!' Lucian rarely lost his temper and Sadie knew she was already walking on thin ice, so she kept quiet. 'You really do need to sort out your head Sadie.'

Luckily three-year-old Amelia had slept through her parent's argument and when Sadie had calmed down she had apologised profusely and made herself and Lucian a hot chocolate. She caught sight of her reflection in the mirror on the landing, her swollen eyes, her face showing her reflection of someone she barely recognised, someone who had suddenly aged ten years over night she noted as she studied her skin and wandered down the stairs in the early hours. She felt an overwhelming deep regret over her recent actions, and she could not stop thinking or feeling guilty about Alora, even though she didn't trust her, however she decided as of today, she would start again and try her best to put things right, she needed to get to the bottom of this mess, and she needed to start with Cassy.

Lucian finally got a couple of hours sleep and still managed his early morning jog which helped clear his mind. After showering he spent a few minutes with Amelia, gave her a kiss and told Sadie that they needed to 'talk tonight to make arrangements.' Sadie didn't like his stern tone; but she was grateful that all three of them were back in the house together. Lucian had tried to make it clear, it was a temporary arrangement, which only gave her the determination she needed to try and save her relationship, which meant rescheduling all her work at her beauty salon and contacting Natalia to take Amelia to nursery. Her plan was to make an extra effort with her appearance and then visit Lucian at work and of course, she would try a different approach, a more subtle approach and even take them a variety of their favourite cakes from the nearby bakery.

'Hi Sadie, I haven't seen you for a while love, how are you?'

'Good thanks Jerry, I was just in town, so I thought I'd pop in and treat Lucian to a cake.'

'Aw you're a good lady, he's a very lucky man, will it be his usual slice of lemon cake?' Jerry asked in his broken English accent, he was close to retiring and had plenty of staff to work for him, however his wife had passed away ten years ago, and he liked to keep busy, and he also had a charming way with the ladies. He beamed as he passed Sadie a slice of her favourite Red Velvet, she knew Cassy would prefer a plain old chocolate éclair and she added a gingerbread man for Amelia too.

Katrina, Lucian's receptionist observed Sadie from the window. She quickly tidied up the papers on her desk without thinking as Sadie had previously commented on the reception desk looking messy. *'Cheeky cow.'* Katrina thought back to when Lucian had awkwardly asked her to tidy her desk about 10 minutes after Sadie had popped in once, *'she had no idea how busy I was that day.'*

Lucian was still in a meeting in his office and had been

for over an hour. He had asked Katrina to not be disturbed unless it was urgent. She wasn't looking forward to telling Sadie this.

'Hiya.' Katrina greeted Sadie with a fake smile while looking at Sadie's box of cakes.

'Hello Katrina, where is he, is he here?' Sadie asked as she continued to march to Lucian's office to the sound of her heels click clicking.

'Yes,' Katrina replied, observing Sadie snooping at the reception desk, judgingly. 'Although, he is in a meeting and cannot be disturbed.'

'Important?'

'I should imagine so,' Katrina refrained from being sarcastic again.

'Yes.'

'I'll have a coffee, while I wait then.'

'You know where the coffee machine is.' Katrina refrained again.

'Black no sugar?'

'Yes please.' Sadie replied looking at her newly manicured nails.

Their small talk was interrupted by the sound of Lucian's giggles followed by a very smartly dressed Mia flicking back her long ash blonde hair in one hand and clutching a folder in the other. Mia smiled confidently as she headed towards both Sadie and Katrina. Sadie mentally compared Mia's cream front slitted suit jacket to her own Dior white single breasted wool and silk bar, it didn't have the welt pockets that very delicately highlighted the waste like hers did, she judged.

The sound of a fake cough by Lucian approached Sadie's direction at reception.

'Hi Sadie' he said in a far too like business manner, as far as Sadie was concerned as Katrina smirked. 'What brings you here?' He had seen her enter via his videocam.

'I was in town, Natalia wanted to take Amelia to nursery and then to the park, so I thought I would pop in and treat you to a cake.'

Sadie was trying to apologise for this morning but was aware of Katrina listening.

'Oh, okay thanks.' Lucian said, in a slightly dismissive tone. 'Where's Cassy?' Sadie asked loud enough to try and get her attention.

'She's in the showroom I think... Lucian paused for a moment, aware of Katrina's presence and guided Sadie to his office. Katrina knew something was going on, Lucian had arrived to work before her, which was unheard of, and with Sadie's surprise visit today, it was all becoming a little suspicious. The tension between them all suddenly heightened as the police officers approached reception.

'Good afternoon, we are looking for Cassy Reynolds.'

The affair

Her

She knew he had felt that too, in that moment the chemistry right there in the room. She had stood closer to him than she normally would, she had purposely leant over his desk and the temperature had risen dramatically. The unease between them had increased as she caught his eyes scanning her breasts then onto her mouth. The sexual tension had created an awkwardness between them where they could no longer be 'just friends.' She felt his glare and was forced to look into his eyes as she straightened her back to try and squeeze past him. He remained still purposely, not letting her. Her impulses were guiding her, until the interruption of the knock on the door.

Him

He didn't know whether that interruption was a blessing or a curse. It was close, very close. He loved this game. He loved remaining professional at work, yet he enjoyed watching her secretly tease him when people were around them. He decided in that moment that he needed to meet her in secret. It was time.

Chapter Ten

Present - London Borough Hospital

'Mrs. Ryan?'

'Hello doctor, call me Jenny, thank you.'

'Jenny, I am Alora's consultant nice to meet you.' The man with the kind face standing in front of Alora's mother Jenny, reminded her of an old schoolteacher that used to teach maths at her secondary school.

'Alora's back surgery was a success, she will need to rest and have some physio, however she is young and otherwise fit and healthy. She has been put into an induced coma for a while to allow her brain to rest as she did receive a bump to her head, her brain activity will be monitored, and I have arranged another scan for later today.

Jenny was pale and the consultant spoke as if reading her thoughts.

'Try not to worry, it's just a precaution as there was some very slight swelling, which could potentially go down, this is sometimes the case and more often than not, so as I say, try not to worry Mrs. Ryan,' he soothed as Jenny took hold of her daughters hand.

Present - London Borough Police Station

Wilson had slept lightly last night and was awoken instantly to the sound of his phone buzzing with a message from Jenkins. He flicked on his coffee machine and noted that it was only 5.33.am. He wasn't due in the station for a few hours; however, Jenkins had some interesting news.

Debra, Wilson's wife, turned over and threw her pillow over her head in a 'do not disturb me if you are going to get up' kind of way. There was just the two of them at home as both their son and daughter had recently flown the nest. Debra was urging Wilson to retire so they could spend more time together. Wilson had thought about retiring often, especially in the last couple of years, however he liked to keep his analytical mind occupied. Jenkins on the other hand lived alone and was 'happy that way,' she declared she had never wanted to marry, and her life revolved around her job and reading, she had very few friends and just a sister that visited her from up north now and again, she loved baking, but preferred working. It was her curiosity that had intrigued her to become a police officer and Wilson could sense the excitement in her message urging him into work early and stating that she would be there within the hour.

Together both Jenkins and Wilson studied the pictures taken form the vehicles. As with any scene in an investigation the first task is to gather any information needed to identify the vehicle and its contents, which starts with an initial and careful examination of the vehicle and what type of evidence may be present. The photographs will then be taken, starting with the exterior from each angle then onto the interior. Afterwards the organised search will commence, which could potentially find items of evidence not observed during the initial examination. D.N.A examinations would be carried out in certain parts of the vehicle and then followed by fingerprints. In this case it was a car accident, which happens daily, however the driver left the scene of an accident, it was assumed that he hadn't been seriously hurt, unlike Alora.

Jenkins produced a letter found in the glove box and handed it to Wilson and waited impatiently for his reaction. Wilson could feel her glare and as usual kept his thoughts to himself and only managed an 'Interesting,' much to Jenkins's annoyance.

The driver over the vehicle had still not been found even though the vehicle was registered to Lucian's business. There had been no identification used to hire the vehicle which was unusual, and there was no D.N.A match or fingerprint match to any of those taken in for questioning. The only description they had, was from Mrs. Petit, who had called for an ambulance. She hadn't remembered what the driver had looked like as she hadn't been wearing her glasses on her dog walk and was very short sighted. Another driver that had found Alora alone, had come forward but there was no actual witness to the accident, which frustrated Jenkins, plus the accident had taken place on an incredibly quiet road leading to the woods.

'Easy for the driver to disappear to the other side of city through the acres of green to the other side of the lake, which is used as a short cut for dog walkers, students, cyclists and joggers. This *is* London. There must be somebody that saw the driver run off or walk or limp if he was injured.'

'Assuming it's a man.' Wilson replied. The car was hired by a woman; the CCTV has shown, and this has been confirmed by Lucian.'

'Yes but it was a man who asked for help from the witness ringing the ambulance for Mrs. Petit.'

'Exactly there's two people perhaps involved already, and we need to keep our options open and arrange investigation at the woods to jog the memories of any regular uses of the area, especially dog walkers etc.'

Wilson read the handwritten letter again before it was handed in for handwriting analysation as he grabbed himself another coffee and replied to his wife Debra.

Blake looked around to see if anyone was watching and pressed the buzzer that was placed at eye level in the old stone walled building that would take him to the third floor for his 11am appointment, the few seconds wait always seemed to be longer than necessary as he waited for the door to open. On entry he pulled his hood back down and took a deep breath and climbed the welcoming staircase and took to the only chair that was sitting outside the room and waited nervously. The door to the right of Blake's chair suddenly opened to the sound of a tickly cough, where a very tall middle-aged man with a thick mass of unruly black hair and hints of grey dressed in a navy suit and a slightly crumpled white shirt welcomed him. 'Blake Preston?' The man's eyebrows rose upwards as he spoke and smiled at Blake in a non-committal way as Blake entered his room. Blake observed the room to be a lot smaller than he had imagined Mr. Collin's room to be, which held the strong scent of coffee, until Mr. Collins opened the window as if to read Blake's mind.

After the formal introduction and a few questions of Blake's date of birth, address etc, Mr. Collins advised Blake to 'try and relax.' 'Why are you here Blake?' Mr. Collins asked as he looked over his glasses and pushed his chair back slightly. Blake initially thought that it was a silly question however he answered with, 'because I need some help.'

'Good.' Mr. Collins sounded pleased as if there was any question as to why Blake was here, but Blake was intelligent enough to realise that maybe some of his clients perhaps would never realise that they needed help. Mr Collins was a top psychiatrist with a long waiting list with great recommendations in the heart of London and wasn't cheap either, and Blake felt himself feeling more relaxed and ready to talk than he had initially anticipated.

'I am being abused.' Blake blurted out, without thinking.

'Okay.' Mr. Collins replied, while making notes. He put the end of his pen onto his chin and asked Blake to be a little more specific, 'who is abusing you Blake?'

'My girlfriend Alora.'

'Okay,' again Mr. Collins answered in a slightly pleased 'we are getting somewhere' tone as he carried on with his notes, however, after a while Blake was able to ignore it.

'She has just been in a car accident and is in a coma at the moment.' Mr. Collins raised his eyebrows again as Blake fidgeted slightly on his chair.

'When you say you are being abused Blake, what do you call abuse?'

'I am being verbally abused, physically abused and she is trying to control me too.'

'And how long has this been going on and how long have you been together, you and Alora?'

'A few years four, five.'

'And how long as she been abusing you Blake?'

'For about the same length of time, four or five years give or take a year.'

'Okay.' Mr. Collins said gently.

'Well, we are here Lor, what do you think, we have walked from Bray to Greystones on this coastal trail, roughly about 6km and look at that view!'

'It's beautiful, and the pebbles are the jewels of the sea, as Aunt Ede always says, I can see why you like Wicklow.'

'Wow you *are* a Geography teacher I'm impressed, lets chill here for a bit and you can continue with your story then we will let your magic map decide where to next.'

Previously.. One year on for Sadie and Lucian, Cassy and Kyle and Alora and Blake.

Dinner Party Two

Menu

Starter
Potted Crab

Main
Soy-lemon flank steak with arugula

Dessert
New York Cheesecake

'Ding Dong.'

'Someone's early, I bet it's the neighbours again.'

'Hi Sophie, hi Tim, you are early, thirty-five minutes in fact, do come in and oh, you have bought little Billy with you, I thought you had a babysitter?'

'Yes, sorry that's why we have arrived early because the babysitter has just bailed out on us, well she said she wasn't feeling well actually, and Billy has been fed so I thought we had better pop in before there were any punch ups!' Sadie was slightly annoyed at Sophie's comment which she made clear by giving Sophie 'a look', however

Sadie wanted to ask Sophie lots of questions, as she was secretly planning her own pregnancy.

'Sophie darling, I take it you are still drinking today, here you go; I have bought your favourite bottle of red,'

'Yes I'm sure I can still have a nice large one!' Sophie beamed.

'Great well, I just wanted to have a word with you if you don't mind, woman to woman and you being a mum as well.' Sadie whispered.

'Oh congratulations!' Sophie replied excitedly and a little too loud for Sadie's liking.

'Oh no' Sadie whispered pulling Sophie towards her and guiding her to the bar stools around the island in the kitchen, I'm not pregnant, not yet anyway, well I don't think I am, well you know, the clock is ticking.'

'Oh okay, so how can I help?' Sophie queried with a look of confusion written all over her face.

'I just wondered if I should start taking folic acid and how quick could it happen if I stopped taking the pill, well between me and you I have already stopped, but don't tell Lucian, she grinned,' I want to surprise him, and also when is the best time to conceive or the best position even? I tried to google it and ..'

'Okay well, I will answer what I can, but I am a breast care nurse not a midwife.'

'I know, but you are a mum too, so that should help.' Sadie ordered.

'Ding Dong.'

'One second Sophie, *Déjà vu* ' Sadie muttered quietly to herself while opening the front door, now officially 'her front door' or more accurately 'their front door' now that she had moved into Lucian's house, and he had added Sadie's name to the property. In front of her stood, Cassy and Kyle, and Lucian's friend Jez and his girlfriend Sarah. She quickly deleted the flashback memory in her mind of the awful introduction of Kyle and Lucian last year, she still wasn't too fond of Kyle, especially being the brother of Lucian's ex Lisa, which was the main reason that she didn't like him around, however Lucian had encouraged her for the sake of *his* employee Cassy, to try and forgive and forget and move on.

'Hi all come on in.'

'Thank you, here you go.'

'Thank you.'

Lucian made an effort to host while cooking and sorted everyone out with beverages, while Sadie sat on the sun lounger ignoring her other guests and read through her notes while interrogating Sophie. Sadie had been reading all about pregnancy and swollen feet and she told Sophie that there was no way she was going to end up wearing 'frumpy sandals' during her pregnancy. Sophie was trying to her best to change the subject whilst trying to keep three-year-old Billy entertained.

'Mum.'

'Mum.'

'One minute Billy.'

'Mum, I don't feel well.'

'What's the matter Billy?'

'I don't feel well mummy it hurts.'

'Have a drink of water Billy, your mummy and I are trying to talk.' Sadie told Billy, much to the annoyance of Sophie as she totally dismissed Sadie's comment and continued to talk to her son.

'Show mummy where it hurts Billy, you do look a bit pale actually.' Billy pulled up his top and pointed to his tummy, and with no notice he leant forwards towards Sadie.

'Aagh! yuk what are you doing!' Sadie screamed as Billy projectile vomited all over Sadie's Jimmy Choo black suede shoes.

'Ding Dong'

Alora and Blake had been running a little late, on entry, they were both welcomed with a distraught Sadie almost in tears about her Jimmy Choo's, while Lucian was telling her to calm down, an embarrassed Sophie was apologising profusely before deciding to take a poorly Billy home.

Alora tried to keep a straight face, not at poor little Billy being sick, more to the fact that he was sick on Sadie's Jimmy Choo's. Her and Sadie were acquaintances more than friends. Sadie was far too high maintenance for Alora, and she would never have befriended her through choice. She wasn't sure if the feeling was mutual, she couldn't tell with Sadie, she didn't really care either, also, Sadie had Blake wrapped around her little finger, whenever she needed him he went running. Alora and Sadie were polite enough to one and other and had socialised together on girl nights out to the cinema and yoga on occasion.

Cassy thought back to one year ago, when Kyle had smacked Lucian, her then new boss, she appreciated the fact that they had all moved on. She was enjoying her newfound friends. She got on well with Sadie and tolerated her more than Alora had at times, and she had now moved in with Kyle, which was something she thought she would never do. Her only concern was Kyle, he never seemed to be completely happy or content. In Cassy's eyes he was the sexiest man she had ever laid eyes on, and also judging by his new followers and groupies that followed him and his band around when he played his bass guitar, so did the mums at the school, they all loved Mr. Bailey

Lucian had gathered everyone around in the conservatory to raise a glass on Blake's request. 'Can we have a little hush please?' Came the request over the sound of the spoons tapping the glasses.

Blake cleared his throat and looked around nervously and thanked everyone for coming, he then asked a bewildered Alora to join him and within seconds Blake had bent down onto one knee and opened a box.

'Alora Ede Ryan will you marry me?' The look on Alora's face told Blake a lot more than he suspected her response ever could, however before she could answer, the doorbell rang. Lucian laughed and joked to Alora to hold that thought as she was 'saved by the bell' while he answered the door. Standing in front of Lucian to his dismay on his doorstep was Lisa, his ex-girlfriend with a baby in her arms.

'Lisa?'

'Yes Lucian it's me Lisa, and this here is your son Louie.'

Lucian tried to force words from his opened mouth, but he was in too much of a state of shock.

'I said this is Louie your son he is 5 months old.'

'Who's at the door Lucian? Sadie shouted marching through the hallway. 'Lisa! What do you want?'

Lisa could not hide her pleasure, watching Sadie eyeing up her and her baby, Lucian's baby, their baby.

'I was telling Lucian, that this here is Louie, he was born in February and Lucian is his father.'

Sadie's mouth formed a perfect O shape. 'What? Ha …right! I would get a paternity, DNA test whatever it's called Lucian, right away, you don't believe that do you?' Sadie awaited a reply from a very pale looking Lucian. 'Lucian, say something, she's clearly lying, do the maths!' Sadie bossed.

'We slept together the night before we split up, didn't we Lucian? The night before your 30th birthday party Sadie, why don't *you* do the maths!' Lisa replied smugly.

Sadie mentally calculated her birthday date 28th May then added nine months to bring her to February.

'Yes, but Lucian told me that you hadn't slept together for months, and you *have* been around the block a little, and well who knows who the father could potentially be.. Lucian, please tell her he's not yours!'

'Is Kyle there? I need to show him his nephew.' Lisa demanded as she pushed past them both through the house onto the garden.

Sophie drew Billy's curtain to block out the sunlight and reached out to close his window, due to the noise that was coming from next door so that he could sleep through the sound of Sadie's voice as it got louder amongst numerous voices trying to calm her down.

'I think we had a lucky escape Billy.' She whispered softly as she stroked his head to sleep.

The drama of Lisa's arrival with baby Louie, had taken priority over Blake's plans, leaving Lucian, Sadie and all their guests stunned. Alora hadn't said yes or no to Blake, however she had felt with Lisa's arrival that she had encountered a lucky escape, she thought selfishly. They had only been together just over a year and by the time they had left the drama at the dinner party and decided to go back to Alora's house she had told Blake that she had been a little bit embarrassed and a little bit annoyed at his proposal which had then led on to an argument.

'What do you mean you were embarrassed? It was just in front of your close family and friends Alora?'

'Exactly, I didn't want an audience, it is meant to be an intimate moment, you know, just me and you preferably?'

'Well, I had another surprise booked, if you had of said yes!'

'I appreciate that but, you know I suppose I would have preferred just us, on a beach or somewhere special or even a picnic in the park would have been a better choice, just not in front of an audience, plus I think it's a little too soon for us.'

'Oh okay, so you say that you would have preferred a

packed-out park or a packed-out beach, yet now you are also saying it's too soon, so now we know the truth!' Blake snapped.

'No, I didn't mean that … I am grateful it's just ..'

'Grateful seriously? It didn't sound like you were..'

'I just didn't want an audience! God, I was just saying …..' Alora was interrupted by the door slamming and Blake leaving.

'Revenge is a dish best served cold. I knew I would get my day.' Lisa muttered to herself as she strapped Louie into his car seat. She had been planning this moment for a few weeks, with the help from Melissa, Sadie's new starter of whom Lisa had befriended through social media.

'Wave goodbye to Uncle Kyle, Louie, I'll be in touch.'

Kyle was waving back proudly to his sister and new nephew. 'I' can't believe I'm an Uncle Cass.'

'Wow, I know but are you sure that Lucian ….'

'Sure, what do you mean am I sure?' Kyle interrupted.

'Well, I mean..'

'You mean you don't believe my sister is telling the truth Cass?'

'No, I didn't say that I just think Sadie had a point.'

'Sadie had a point. What do you mean by that?' Kyle questioned.

'About Lucian being the father.'

'Oh, right okay I get it..'

'No, I'm not I was just saying… Kyle where are you going, wait for me please.'

'I'm not staying here; I need to clear my head.'

'Oh god, get rid of your parents please?' Sadie begged.

'I can't, they have only just arrived, and they saw Lisa drive off with the baby, she had messaged my mum apparently and told them they were grandparents.'

'Good god, well we don't even know if he is your baby yet not for sure!'

'Well, I'd like to talk to my dad Sadie, hang on please let me process this.'

'Go to their house then if you want to talk about your make-believe son, if not, I'm leaving!'

'Well, did she say yes?' Blake answered his phone by accident, he had wanted to decline his incoming call.

'Well?' Blake's mum asked eagerly.

'What, oh okay mum hi, and no not yet I haven't done it yet, I'll call you later.' He lied and hung up abruptly.

Sonia looked at her phone strangely as if it was doing the talking itself. Blake hadn't sounded very happy at all, and she wondered what Alora had done this time. She wasn't too keen on Alora if the truth be told, she had hoped that Blake may eventually get back with his ex-wife Ann, mainly because she was the mother of his children and she believed that children were better off with both parents remaining together, whatever the circumstances. Unbeknown to Blake, Sonia had been messaging Ann and keeping her up to date with Blake's new business, new home, the fact that Blake had stopped drinking and gambling, and anything else that she could say that would perhaps bring them back together, in which had almost worked until Alora had come along. 'Miss career woman Alora' she called her to her husband Peter, who had never really listened to Sonia's moaning and had once told her to stop being such a hypocrite and to stop interfering.

Peter had two daughters and a son from a previous marriage, however Blake was Sonia's only birth child and her life revolved around him. Secretly she had hoped that Alora would decline his offer of his hand in marriage, she didn't trust her, she was far too pretty to be trusted, Sonia had told Peter.

'Jeez these dinner parties' are not going too well are they, I'd give up on the next one!' Johnny joked.

'Johnny you laugh at everything, you always have!' Alora tried hard to sound stern, but it was hard for her to be serious now that she was here with Johnny.

'Well, ya know, it's like one of them soaps me ma used to make us all sit through at seven o'clock every night. I'd pretend I was interested so I could stay up, mind you like your stories in the end I wanted to know what happened next like I do now, anyway what was with the proposal? Did you say yes or no? It didn't sound like it went down too well, come on fill me in would ya.'

'Well, that is where it started to go wrong, for all of us, Johnny.'

The affair

Him

'Hey.'

Her

'Hiya, you ok?'

Him

'No not really, sorry she has really annoyed me, sorry I know she's your friend, but she can be hard work sometimes.'

Her

'That's ok I know she has no filter haha.'

Him

'Anyway, don't worry, have you heard from her?'

Her

'No nothing since the dinner party earlier, if it's any consolation me and him have had words as well again.'

Him

'Oh no sorry to hear that, Lisa turning up with the baby has almost topped last year's dinner party.'

Her

'I know I did actually think that haha, sorry I shouldn't laugh.'

Him

'That's ok,' he smiled, 'anyway what brings you here?'

Her

'Well, I have come to speak to the landlord,, my friend wants to hold a christening in the back room. I was going to pop in tomorrow, but after the drama earlier at the dinner party, I decided I needed to get out and fancied a walk to clear my head.'

Him

And your feet bought you here, 'he smiled. Do you want a drink?'

Her

'Yes a lemonade no ice would be nice please thanks.'

Him

'I will have the same I think, I have drunk enough today.'

Her

'Are you going to the opening of 'The Palace' the new nightclub in a couple of weeks, four weeks tomorrow I think it is on the 17th?'

Him

'Yes meant to be,' he said as he paid for the drinks, 'we have tickets for all six of us that's probably what we all need, a good night out eh, do you want me to get that stall for you and bring it to the bar?'

Her

'Yes okay then,' she slips off her coat and pops her bag down, 'things still not good for you two then and did you ask her about you know what you said you was going to ask her? And if it's any consolation when we met up the other night she didn't mention another guy.'

Him

He tried a small smile. 'That's something I suppose, thanks.'

With the combination of both their hurt, anger and alcohol consumption, there was only one way tonight was going.

Chapter Eleven

The morning after Dinner Party Number two.

'I bet your head is sore this morning Lucian!' Sadie said angrily as she pushed his arm away from herself as she woke up, she was furious with Lucian after he had strolled in after midnight, even though she had only been home just thirty minutes herself.

'Typical you Sadie, it's all about you, what about me for once eh? I was only told yesterday that I was a father, it was a bit of a shock to the system you know, I wasn't planning on having any kids just yet.' Lucian replied angrily as he got out of bed and thrown on his dressing gown.

'And what about my feelings? Maybe I *do* want to have kids sooner rather than later!' Sadie shouted at the slammed door behind Lucian who was well on his way down to the kitchen coffee machine. He really could not be doing with her crap today he thought and google searched the words D.N.A test.

Sadie anxiously looked for Lucian's phone in the bedroom until she realised he had taken it with him downstairs. *'Mmm he's clearly got something to hide, maybe he was with her last night, the so-called mother of*

his child, Lisa!'
A little while after when Sadie had calmed down, she decided that she would take a different route from now on. She sat and thought for a few minutes and after doing a full 360-degree circle she then decided, she would find out the truth and play the game, instead of getting angry. She would become the supporting little girlfriend that Lucian wanted her to be. She unblocked Lisa from her social media and after some interesting discoveries she then decided to go and apologise to Lucian, after she ordered a tracking device and threw away her pill.

Cassy sighed as she took the spare quilt from Kyle's sofa and placed it back in the cupboard. It had been the sound of the shower that had woken her this morning when she found herself alone in Kyle's bed. He had had now gone out, without even saying goodbye or good morning even. He still hadn't been home just after midnight when she had checked, so it could have been the early hours for all she knew. She wondered how Alora was after yesterday, she would normally contact her, but she really wasn't in the mood today and hid under her quilt and planned on not doing a lot for the rest of the day.

The pain in Blake's neck was a reminder of his drunkenness which had led him to sleep on his sofa. The taste of stale alcohol on his breath accompanied by the dulling ache in his head filled him with immediate regret and disappointment towards himself. He hadn't touched a drop of alcohol for over a year until yesterday.

He had lost control and now he was gutted. Alora had rejected his proposal and he couldn't handle it, his heart sank. The sudden realisation that it was Saturday, and he was collecting his children at midday, snapped him out of his self-pity for a moment as he noted the time. He fumbled for his phone and noted two missed calls from Alora and a voicemail. She hadn't changed her mind about the proposal, by the sound of the message, which angered him slightly. He needed to get back in control, he was having his kids today so Alora could stew for a bit he thought as he started to tidy up. She had rejected him, and it was partially her fault that he had drank so she could wait, he decided.

Alora had started to regret yesterday's events as soon as she had woken up far too early at the crack of dawn, and now she felt tired and wanted to go back to bed. She wondered how Blake was after their argument, although he hadn't bothered to ring or message her. She had left a soppy sorry message in the early hours, and now she was regretting her apology, slightly. She had only been honest, and she hadn't ruled out marriage completely, but they had only been dating a year and there were issues in which she wanted them to address. A wave of panic overcame her suddenly as she studied her pale face in her dressing table mirror as she brushed her neglected golden hair. She had hoped he hadn't started drinking after their row yesterday, he had done so well. The thought of him drinking terrified her, however in that moment a notification from Blake appeared on her phone.

'I got your message, I have the kids today and tonight, I will talk to you tomorrow. B.'

'Oh well, he's okay then thank god,' she thought relieved. *'Still no mention of am I okay or anything, no kiss on his message and no apology for his temper.'* 'Okay.'

A day to herself is what she needed and after pottering about for a while she, decided to go for a drive and sit on her favourite quiet place on the hill, where her and her first love Johnny used to sit.

'Aw the hill Alora, I remember it well, we had some fun their didn't we.' Johnny teased.

Alora smiled but her eyes were showing sadness.

'Hey, no emotion, it means I'm losing you, Alora. Alora, don't go back yet!'

Present - London Borough Hospital

The consultant was pleased today with Alora's progress. She had shown a 'glimpse of awareness', for a moment. Her mechanical ventilation will now be reduced as will the sedation medication as the brains activity that has been closely monitored is showing a positive progress.

'We shall adjust the level of drugs accordingly, to ensure the brain remains in a state of rest. Well done.'

'That's better come on, tell me more of the story later, I want to go and see me ma.'

'Okay then yes Johnny let's go. Bless your mum she is still so beautiful.' Alora observed as she looked at the photo of Johnny's mother and her grandchildren on the mantel piece.'

'Of course, she is where do you think I get my looks from eh?' Johnny said only half joking.

He wasn't wrong Alora thought, admiringly, they were a lovely looking family and Johnny had his mums looks alright. Johnny rarely talked about his father, he had died a few years ago. Johnny had never been that close to him when he was a child either. He always seemed to be working away a lot and when he was home, he would like a drink and lose his temper.

Alora reflected back to when she had witnessed Johnny's father's temper when they had first started dating and he had turned on Johnny for sticking up for his mum. His dad was fairer than Johnny and his hair was fine, Johnny had inherited his mum's dark thick locks and he really did have eyes that smiled, an emerald green 'that matched the emerald isle.' As his ma always joked.

'You were wrong about her watching her soaps though Johnny,' Alora whispered, 'she's not here is she?' The room was full of pictures of all of her kids and of what Alora assumed was her grandchildren. The house was dated, some might say old fashioned, yet, spotlessly clean, with manicured lawns and acres of land.

'No, she must be out, let's go and check on grandma.'

'Oh yeah where is she?'

'She'll be in the kitchen rocking on her chair, looking out of the window and watching the world go by I bet.'

'Bless her, she can't hear us can she Johnny?'

'No, don't be silly of course she can't, but I bet she can

feel our presence though, you know like when she used to say when she could feel my grandpa's presence. There she is rocking on her chair, looking out of the window at the world and nature with her music on, she never watches tv, she never has, she has dementia now bless her and she just sings all her old favourite tunes.

'Aw bless her she is so sweet.' Alora gushed.

'Isn't she bless her and she can still sing a tune too. Come on let's go and explore the grounds before the sun goes down.'

'Yeah it's a gorgeous evening Johnny.. I was just thinking ...'

'Don't do that it's not good.'

'Haha well, do you get like seasons in heaven, you know like Spring, Summer, Autumn, Winter?' 'No not really, we just have these blue skies, and we don't know the temperature because we don't feel it. There is no rain or snow if that's what you mean. to answer your question Alora, there are no seasons here in heaven Alora and there are no seasons in love either.'

'Aw you old romantic you Johnny.'

'I know that's me, and you know from what you have told me so far it all seems a bit of a mess, or it was for you back home, with your life and Blake, although you have only told me half the story so far, but me and you we had fun, we laughed, I know we were young, but you and that Blake and your friends, well what you have got to ask yourself is, were any of you, or are any of you with the right one. Life is short and well I know that, and we only get one shot, and now you are here with me, only halfway mind, I think you will have a choice to go back, your not fully fledged like me, but you got here because your life was such a mess, so if there is one thing I want to do is sort things out with you and together we will find out how you got here, if you want me to help you I will, but relationships you have to work on them you really do.'

Alora was in deep thought, she started to think of Blake and her life, her parents and her family and friends and while she was here she could forget her life back home for a while, she was having too much fun she thought without any guilt at all, no full emotion currently and she quite enjoyed it, she laughed with Johnny, but it was different back home, her life had been a bit of a mess she knew that, but it just seemed like a distant memory. 'Yes, you're right let's have some fun here, Johnny.' 'Too right sweetheart, come on don't be thinking, let's go to me local, McCarthy's.'

'Ha Johnny, you say 'me local' like you never left the place.'

'Well home is where the heart is Alora and mine is here, with you.'

'Well, it's lively enough and that band is really getting the party going.'

'They sure are, looks like it's going to be one good night.'

'Everyone is dressed so smartly Johnny.'

'Of course, they are, they are paying their respects to

a good old local guy that used to drink in here and celebrating his life.'

'Oh gosh is this a wake Johnny?' Alora asked in disbelief as the sound of the Irish music filled the air.

'Yes my love this is how we do it here, come on let's dance.'

'Wow Johnny what fun this is.'

'You still got the moves you really have; I know almost everyone in here, shame I can't introduce you to them properly and myself, but hey we can dance like no one's watching Alora because they are not haha!'

'Haha Johnny you make me laugh. I have been to duller weddings than this Johnny, what a way to celebrate one's life.'

'I know it's some craic eh, all my favourites tunes too.'

'Well to whoever's life we are celebrating, here's to you.'

'Yes, may he have eternal peace and be in no more pain, here is to you fella.'

'Aw Johnny just look at that beautiful butterfly.'

Johnny felt an enormous sense of love tonight, the first time he had felt any emotion, sat in the corner was a lady who was surrounded by her friends and family, she had been alternating between tears of sorrow and tears of joy as she joined in with some of the band's tunes. Johnny smiled to himself as a man took her in his arms and held the tall darked haired lady and kissed her gently. The love here tonight was in the air and in a quiet moment he took a deep breathe, pushed Alora's golden locks away from her face and kissed her.

The affair

Her

She still could not forget that kiss. She had tried, oh she had tried. It had meant something. It still means something. That kiss was not a silly kiss. It was not just a silly kiss, not to her. She had never been kissed like that before, never and she needed to be kissed like that again. The softness of his mouth, the warmness of his tongue had left her feeling euphoric then and the thought of him kissing her like that again had encouraged her feelings. She wanted him and hopefully he wanted her. There was no rationale for such behaviour, for hers or for his. Without the kiss she was still being unfaithful with her constant thoughts of him. She had given up trying at home, she had been neglected, hurt and she had cried, and now, she didn't care and deep down she didn't think her 'friend' cared too. She had confided in her and told her that she wasn't sure where they were going. She used those words to ease her own conscious. Surely he deserved better. He needed someone that was sure where they were going and so did she. He was clearly thinking the same she realised a message notified her phone.

'Do you want to meet? x'

Him

He found himself thinking of her, she had been quite sweet about the whole kiss thing. He had felt a bit sorry for her, she had seemed as lost as he was and at least she hadn't made a big drama about telling his girlfriend, her 'friend' about that kiss. He loved sex and she was still making excuses at home; she knew he had a huge sex drive, and it was so selfish on her part. He needed sex; all relationships need sex. He was still none the wiser as to whether she was sleeping with someone else. He had followed her, checked her phone and done all he could do other than ask her out right. He had no proof, only his friend saying he saw her in the car with another man and of course the obvious current sexless relationship at home. She had been busy with work though, so how would she find the time? It made him want her more, her at home, if there was someone else fighting for her affection. As for her friend if it all went wrong he would have her. She was cute and they got on well, and he guessed she would be wild in bed. Maybe he could have them both? Just a thought, worth a try though. He smiled as he received a reply.

'Yes, where and when? x'

Chapter Twelve

Alora's eyes were half open in desire and her body felt relaxed as she responded to Johnny's soft mouth. He kissed her like she had never been kissed before and it was in that moment she felt the promise of realness and yet the world itself ceased to exist as he placed his hands gently in her hair until she felt protected. No words were needed or spoken until the end of the wake where they sang and danced until the last of the regulars were stumbling out of McCarthy's.

'Well, that was some Craic Alora, where next?'

'Johnny I haven't dance like that in ages.'

'Alora I haven't been kissed like that in ages.'

'Johnny, it was lovely, but it's weird I could feel everything, and being here as I call it .. halfway to heaven, I wasn't feeling any emotion, feeling passion anything but now, after we kissed, well...'

'Hey Alora, don't over think it it's purely love, that's what it is, it happened, and truth be told I never stopped loving you, I know we were young but..'

'Really Johnny? I suppose I do feel the same, I mean I wouldn't have kissed you back would I if I didn't feel the same and if I still loved Blake, I wouldn't kiss anybody else would I?' Johnny shook his head in agreement.

'Was there not anyone here in Ireland that you loved Johnny?' Alora awaited Johnny's response.

'Yes there was someone quite recent, well no I mean recently as in before I died, but anyway less of that, it's another story and I will tell you about it at some point, but for now let's get back to you, where was we, and why did you turn down Blake's proposal, don't tell me it was too soon that won't wash with me.'

'Okay Johnny where was I.'

'You were on the hill where me and you use to hang out.'

'Yes that's right, do you know what Johnny we should go there now, do you fancy it? Maybe we could see what is going on back in England with everyone.'

'Well yeah we could go to the hill, I'm not sure about going to see your friends yet, maybe after you have told me the full story Alora.'

The hill was as Johnny remembered it, minus the temperature it was a beautiful sunny day and there was only the two of them perched on top of the hill, it brought back fond memories for them both. They both rolled down the hill like they had done as children only this time with no cuts and grazes, yet still laughing hysterically. They lay at the bottom until Alora decided it was time to open up to Johnny. 'So yes the proposal.'

'Oh yeah so why turn him down apart from the fact that you had only been together just over a year and the setting wasn't quite right, I know you better than that Alora, come on spill.'

'Okay I will.'

Blake decided to message Alora when he had dropped his children off, the feeling of the fading hangover wanted to take him to bed. He had put on a great front today, in front of his children, he didn't want to admit to them or himself or to anyone ever, that he had given in to the temptation of alcohol yesterday, after he had abstained for so long. He wanted to be back in control. His children 11-year-old Sky and 9-year-old Ben had asked after Alora, they liked her, and this had saddened him. After her reaction and his reaction and the mess he had made of the weekend, it definitely had not gone to his plan, instead he made an excuse as to why Alora hadn't been around.

Alora had enjoyed her own company today, in fact a lot better than she had anticipated than she would. She made her own dinner for one and chose to cook the way she wanted to a chicken alfredo pasta bake. Blake had an intolerance to pasta and didn't even like Alora cooking it for herself. Blake could never leave her be in the kitchen alone either, he was always telling her what knife to use or how much or how little spice to add. At first she found it quite helpful and quite endearing until one night she had added red wine into her casserole dish without thinking and Blake had tasted it as he had tried to control what spices he thought she needed to add before she could warn him, and the evening had ended in a huge argument. So today she had enjoyed cooking and eating her dinner alone, in front of the television, while watching an old black and white romantic film, in fact it was one of her favourite old-time classics that she had watched lots of times as a child with her Great Aunt Ede.

She had been closer to her Great Aunt Ede more so than her own Grandma and Grandad, they were still around and very young at heart and spent most of their retirement travelling the world, especially escaping the winters in England, they always liked to travel to a warmer climate.

After dinner Alora cleaned up and decided to stretch out on her sofa, she switched off her phone and watched he old black and white romantic classic for two hours and nine minutes, and at the end she shed a tear for her Great Aunt Ede after losing her just recently.

Blake would never watch a romantic film with her, and she found herself sitting through hours of football or history programmes, at a push she preferred the latter. When she confided to her mum about 'such a petty thing' her mum's words in her reply had stated that 'that's just men for you.' Alora wanted more, she wanted romance for ever. 'Your head is in the clouds love.' Her mother would say as her father sat their watching 'his programmes.' Alora knew what she wanted and needed all her boxes ticked before she made any rash decisions, hence the reasons Blake's proposal didn't go to plan. She had also been so busy with her job lately and had a chance to apply for head teaching assistant recently and Blake hadn't appeared to be very happy about it at the time and suggested that she may end up with too much work on her hands in the evenings and weekends, which meant less time for 'them.'

Sadie flushed her contraceptive pills down the toilet and waited patiently for the tracker she had ordered to arrive. She had already decided where she was going to place it in Lucian's car. She had researched 'top tracking devices' and decided on one that would ring her mobile if there was any sound, so therefore *if* he was playing away, and tried to have a discreet conversation she would hear it all. She hadn't realised what she was doing was illegal until she had searched it. Still, her need to keep tabs on Lucian overpowered any rational thinking. It had all been a bit of a mess after the dinner party on Friday night after Lucian's disappearance, and, she had been foolish herself, however she would now play the dutiful girlfriend and hopefully become the mother of Lucian's baby herself and perhaps his dutiful wife, and with her determined nature and great tenacity she would find out the truth. She liked to be in control and her feelings for Lucian had scared her sometimes, but either way she wanted a baby she was thirty-one now and it was her time to be a mum. *'Fuck Lisa'* she thought bitterly.

Lucian was a bit confused; Sadie had been acting weird all day, she was acting just a little too nice. She had cooked him his favourite 'lamb roast' even though she couldn't stand it herself, and for dessert his favourite Banoffee pie. She had also spoken about Louie in an affectionate way, like she had accepted him already and that she had believed that he *was* Lucian's child. She had cleaned all the house before dinner, applied full make up and lit some candles and offered him a back massage to get him 'in the mood.'

Lucian decided he would just embrace it all, for today anyway, he wasn't silly, Sadie was clearly up to something, however today he was enjoying the peace. He needed his head clear after the weekend, and he also needed to know if he was the father to Louie. Having kids was certainly not in his plan at the moment.

Lucian took off his shirt and let Sadie do her thing and let all his tension slip away. They went to bed soon after and Sadie's plan to fall pregnant without consulting Lucian had been put into action.

Cassy had never known Kyle to be so distant. He hadn't even asked her how she was or apologised for the way he had left her stranded at the dinner party. In fact, he had barely spoken at all. She had only suggested that Lisa his siter maybe lying about the father of her baby, but she soon learnt the way to upset Kyle was to say something about his sister, he was so protective, maybe it was because they only had each other, no parents, only some distance cousins in Ireland. Cassy knew she had hit a raw nerve and when she did try to apologise he had cut her short with, 'forget it, I don't want to talk about it.' Either way he was an uncle. The only thing he had mentioned today about the weekend was Blake's proposal. *'Why was he so bothered?'* Cassy thought to herself. He seemed to always be interested in Alora lately or what Alora and Blake was or wasn't doing. Cassy never broached the subject, but she wasn't stupid and that was mainly the reason she had moved in with Kyle, or 'gate crashed his house,' like Kyle had worded it to her one day. She had been sick of listening to Kyle and Alora talking every time Kyle had visited her when she lived at Alora's. As long as she kept them two apart the more she would try and get Kyle to feel the way about her that she did about him. Cassy knew that Alora wasn't entirely to blame, although at times she resented her.

Kyle had mixed emotions, he wasn't happy at the moment with Cassy, in fact he had never been truly happy with Cassy. He liked her of course he did, but he didn't love her like she proclaimed to love him. She always said the wrong thing, she had no filter, and she could be really childish sometimes. He had been so happy to have been told he was an uncle to baby Louie yesterday and had visited his sister today. Lisa had told Kyle that she had messaged Lucian and that he had requested a D. N. A test which she was happy to provide. She insisted that Lucian was definitely the father to Louie, as she hadn't been near anyone other than Lucian. Kyle had questioned Lisa and told her that it would be morally wrong to lie about the situation, as her brother, she allowed him to question her, but no one else could, she had listened, and he had believed her.

'Do you want to go The Bull tonight for a drink?'
Alora thought for a moment and noted the 'no kiss' before replying. *'Hi Blake, maybe it's just well you know Monday night first day back at work, a pile of marking but I could do tomorrow night?'* She replied with no kiss.

Blake didn't like *her* reply without the kiss and thought bitterly for a moment before he replied, until his thoughts were disturbed by a delivery driver delivering some parts at his garage.

'Cheers mate.'

'Okay maybe, I may be busy though tomorrow night you know in case I have to have the kids'

He never has the kids on a Tuesday night, Alora thought. She hesitated for a moment and re read his message. *'Okay then maybe Wednesday?'* Even if he was just being awkward, she would still be polite, but with no kiss. Alora didn't receive a reply until 9pm on Tuesday evening. *'You are silly, Alora toy could have had iit all wit me, and you turn my down. 'Oh no Blake,'* she thought, *'you had been doing so well,'* She rang him straight away as soon as she realised he had been drinking and on the fourth time her call got declined so she texted him.

'Blake please don't drink, wherever you are I will pick you up, ring me now!' She decided to drive to The Bull in desperation, she parked on the taxi rank outside in her haste and heard a driver shouting something to her. He wasn't there, she then drove to The Six bells, he wasn't in there either. She spotted one of Blake's football mates coming out of the gent's toilets as she was leaving.

'You have just missed him love, just got in a taxi, in a right state said he was going to yours.'

'Okay thank you. 'Alora raced home as fast as she could drive within the speed limit and just about managed to dash through a red light without causing an accident.

She pulled up at home and found a hunched-up figure on her doorstep. 'Come on let's get you inside,' struggling she eventually managed to help Blake onto her sofa. He sat with his head in his hands without saying a word as Alora made him a strong coffee. She grabbed a packet of biscuits to add some sugar for him. 'Here you are, get these down you and I've put extra milk in the coffee for you.'

'Smack!' The coffee mug smashed straight onto Alora's oak fireplace mirror, and the remains of the coffee followed.

'What are you doing Alora? Please stop! Why did you just throw that mug of coffee at me? You are crazy woman, it just missed me you have broken your favourite mirror too, what is wrong with you?' Blake's pleads were ignored as Alora froze on the spot.

'You are a horrible spoilt little princess and you have made me drink; this is all your fucking fault; you waste of space!'

'Blake! Stop it, why are you saying those nasty things?' Alora pleaded shockingly as her hands started to tremble and in that moment she wasn't sure if she wanted to follow him or let him go as he slammed her front door. In her state of shock, she chose the latter after she had initially pleaded with him to come back.'

She felt sick, she wasn't sure of what just happened, but all she could hear was Blake's insults over and over again. After poring herself a glass of water, she decided to lock her front door and ring Cassy.

'Cassy don't ask any questions and please don't tell

anyone, but it's Blake he is drunk, and he has just come round here and was horrible to me. He won't listen to me, could you ask Kyle please to drive to mine and pick him up please?' Alora asked desperately.

'Oh no are you okay? Did he hurt you? Don't worry I will ask him now.'

Kyle looked as if he had fallen asleep in front of the television when Cassy entered the bedroom, however he woke upon her entry half hearing her phone call, Cassy wasn't the quietest.

'It's okay Kyle don't worry it's nothing.' Cassy didn't want Kyle helping Alora, however, she wanted to help her so she decided to drive to Alora's house herself. She grabbed her raincoat and ran her fingers through her hair in the hall mirror before leaving. As she reversed out of Kyle's drive to the sound of a crunch, she realised that she caught the side of one of his lights, which delayed her slightly.

'Cassy? It's me you ok? Has Kyle left yet? Only he's banging on my door and..'

'Ok don't panic Alora, just ignore the door, help is on his way.' Cassy hadn't noticed Kyle watching her from the bedroom window. He had heard her say something about Alora and Blake and had also heard the crunch and after checking his car he headed off to Alora's house.

Sadie missed the first sound of the tracker calling as she hadn't wanted to take her phone in the shower, and after she had dried off the tracker called her again.

'Oh my god, it works!' Sadie whispered to herself then immediately put her phone on mute.

Sadie had set the tracking equipment to be able to listen in on any call that Lucian made. She desperately wanted to be able to listen in on any call he had received but hadn't quite been able to work that part out and she couldn't ask for help from anyone, she couldn't tell anyone about this little device.

'Cass? you okay, I had a missed call?'
The sound of windscreen wipers, an indicator of a car and the low *noise* of some music was all Sadie could hear, until Cassy's voice became clear.

'Oh, hi Lucian thanks for ringing back, hang on let me pull over.'

Sadie was amazed at how this gadget actually worked.' *Jeez it really does work, come on spill I can't wait to hear this, why should Cassy be ringing Lucian unless it's work related though?'* Sadie thought with a combination of feeling amazed and annoyed in equal measure.

'Sorry Lucian I didn't know who else to ring.'

'What's up Cass?' *'Ooh Cass is it now, how friendly!'* Sadie's irrational jealousy never relented as she muttered to herself. 'It's Alora I don't know what's happened with her and Blake, but I think he's had a drink and well, she sounds scared I am just pulling back up to the house now, I went there first but couldn't get hold of either of them, so I drove around for a while and I'm a bit worried because neither of them are answering their phones and Alora was really upset when she rang.'

'Oh right, shit well where's Kyle did he not come with you?' Lucian asked.

'Exactly Lucian thank you, why is she ringing you, where

the fuck is Kyle? And Blake, you stupid idiot.' Sadie was asking the same question of Kyle's whereabouts along with her genuine concern for Blake.

'He was asleep when Alora rang me.'

'Okay well, call him now, stay in the car outside Alora's and I will drive to Blake's and follow his path to back to where you are, ok?'

'Okay thanks.' Cassy totally ignored Lucian's advice and headed towards Alora's front door, she checked for the spare front door key under the ceramic pot, it was gone. *'Weird,'* Blake had a key to Alora's. The front door was unlocked, the hall light on and Alora's coat lay on the floor, along with her phone.

'Sade?'

'I have just had a call from Cassy, who's had a call from Alora, and Blake's on the drink and they can't find him, do you want to come with me I said I will help?'

'I like the honesty,' Sadie thought. Obviously, she already knew all this but had to remain unaware.

'Oh no! Okay silly fool, and yes I am just getting dressed give me two minutes.'

Cassy felt a wave of panic, seeing Alora's coat on the floor with her phone next to it, she did not know what to expect. She entered the lounge and her eye caught site of the long crack on Alora's oak mirror together with splashes of brown all over her fireplace and on the floor with the broken peach coloured mug. She didn't want to touch it, she thought as her imagination started working overtime, *'this could be a crime scene.'* As fear started to overtake her, she walked slowly to the kitchen terrified of what she may find. Nothing. She grabbed a knife and tiptoed quietly up the stairs. A creak on the stair almost giving her away until she heard muffled voices coming from Alora's bedroom. She took a deep breath and pushed opened Alora's bedroom door. She felt sick.

'What are *you* doing here? She asked Kyle, and why are you two in the bedroom?' Her eyes turned to Alora, and her voice pretended to be a lot calmer than her actual feelings.

Both Alora and Kyle looked at Cassy as though she had two heads. It took a moment for Cassy to realise she still had the large knife in her hand, so she stomped back down the stairs making a noise like a child stamping its feet having a tantrum, she headed towards the kitchen and placed the knife neatly back into its stand.

She walked out the front door and lit a cigarette and decided to ring Lucian.

'It's okay Lucian, no sign of Blake here at Alora's and Kyle's here cosying up to Alora in her bedroom.'

Lucian was already at Alora's front garden gate, fiddling with it, it had an awkward latch. He saw Cassy and hung up and she flicked up the latch.

Lucian looked at her quizzically, unsure of what to stay until Cassy flung herself into his arms. 'Hey, come on don't be silly,' he managed as Kyle appeared on the front doorstep. Lucian then explained that Sadie had spotted Blake walking alongside the bushes at the last junction and was going back to look for him. Sadie wasn't frightened of Blake, he was her brother's best friend after all, and she had three of them who would always protect her, besides she cared about him deeply and Sadie rarely cared about anyone else before herself, but tonight she was genuinely worried, and she wouldn't give up until she had found him.

'Wow, just wow Lor, what a horrible piece this Blake guy is, please tell me you left him, or he had a head transplant for god's sake Alora Ryan he is a shit you deserve better, and you and Kyle in the bedroom? I take he was just helping you?' Johnny asked concerned as he held her closely hugging her.

'The only true apology is changed behaviour; actions speak louder than words. If you don't see any change? There was never an apology to begin with.'

The affair

Her

She could still feel the embrace of his arms around her, and it that moment she felt safe from the world. It was more than a friendly hug she decided which had made her feel warm inside. His physical touch along with his soft scent of a hint of his aftershave as she inhaled, had relaxed her deeply as she felt his warm breath close to hers. There was a moment that hug could have turned into a kiss, again. It hadn't not tonight, not after all the drama. She hadn't felt that sense of what a hug could mean from anyone else before and she didn't think she would feel it again and convinced herself that she wasn't reading into it either. She had tried to fight it, but her feelings for him had started to run deep. This wasn't a silly little schoolgirl crush, and she hadn't chosen her feelings, but something was happening between them, and it was powerful, and he was on her mind still as she lay there with her head on the pillow until she finally fell into a deep sleep.

Him

In that moment when they had hugged, he had genuinely felt something. It wasn't about him finding her attractive or the thought of her being his girlfriend's friend that gave him a buzz of excitement because of his high sex drive, he had genuinely felt that she cared for him and had needed him. He respected her and he respected his girlfriend too, but him and his girlfriend they were not right at the moment. She just did not get him, he thought bitterly. Yet the hug tonight with her felt natural and now the confusion really did start to set in as he encountered mixed emotions and had actually started to feel something more than just a need for sex, he had started to need her too.

Chapter Thirteen

Previously

Blake woke up freezing, the dampness of the morning mildew on his face. It was a fresh morning for early September, and the last few days had past him in a blur. The smell of stale beer on his breathe every morning was becoming far too familiar. This was his wake-up call. He was a mess; and had been in a vicious circle. He couldn't even remember last night. He pulled himself up from the wet ground and noticed the blue skies of a beautiful sunny morning. An elderly lady approached him with what appeared to be a friendly little apricot poodle.

'Come here Ruby.'

The elderly dog walker's loud voice and the yap of the dog pounded Blake's head. He managed to swap pleasantries before heading back home. After what would have normally been a fairly short walk had Blake been feeling okay, had taken him a lot longer as he had to stop on more than one occasion. When he finally approached his front door, the smell of musty air, combined with half empty cans of alcohol greeting him, halted him in his tracks. *'This has to stop I need to sort myself out now.'*

After a tidy up a very strong coffee and a shower, Blake searched the internet for some help, he needed to open up, he needed to tell the truth. After a lengthy search, he finally found a recommend therapist called Mr. Collins, however there appeared to be quite a long queue for his services which could mean a long wait, he started his search again as he lay on his sofa until he fell into a much-needed deep sleep instead.

One-week later Alora and Blake arranged to meet and at their regular coffee shop in town, Alora's choice, a day before Alora's birthday. Blake had kindly bought Alora a new mirror for her birthday and Alora was a little embarrassed as she opened it while they both sat in the in the corner.

Alora was pleased to hear that Blake was approaching day eight of staying sober. She had pecked him on the cheek as she had left and had agreed to take things slowly, still living apart, for now. It would be a test for him this weekend at the V.I.P opening at the Palace, it would be the first time where all six of them would be together in a while. Blake continued throwing himself into work and accepted that things needed to change, he was no longer going to be a victim he decided, he needed to be strong.

Sadie felt both excitement and dread in equal measures every time the tracker rang, she had now managed to work the gadget so that she could hear both Lucian's

incoming and outgoing calls as well as is his location. She hadn't heard anything interesting since the night, Lucian had gone to Alora's house. *'It's okay Lucian, no sign of Blake here at Alora's and Kyle's here cosying up to Alora in her bedroom!'*
Sadie hadn't heard the rest of the story but Alora and Kyle? She knew she had been right about them two all along, however Blake had been her priority and not long after that she found him in a terrible state, and they had talked for hours, and she had comforted him.

Sadie wasn't as convinced that it was as innocent as Lucian had assumed with Alora and Kyle and he had also stated that he thought Cassy may have 'overreacted.' Sadie had seen the way Kyle acted around Alora and, Cassy had also confided in Sadie about her fears too. The problem for Sadie now was how Cassy had started to confide in Lucian every time she was vulnerable, and it appeared that they no longer just had a relationship as employee and her boss, however for the past couple of weeks she had decided that today would be the last day of her tracking, but it was almost becoming an addiction and she needed to know what Lucian was up to. He had been so distant since the dinner party after Lisa had turned up. He was still waiting on D.N.A results which she assumed would arrive via the post any time soon. The tracker number rang just as Lucian had left the house and was barely on the drive.

'Phew that was close.' Sadie sighed with relief.

'Hi Cassy, you okay?'

'Yes thanks, well no, I just wondered, I know it's short

notice sorry but, I have decided to move out of Kyle's for a bit and I don't want to go back to Alora's and there is a flat that I can view and …'

'You would like the day off?' Lucian interrupted.

'Yes please.'

'Should be fine, as long as you have no important appointments then yes, just sort yourself out love okay.'

'Love? Love now is it?' Sadie thought bitterly.

'Thank you Lucian, you are the best.' Sadie noticed the change of tone in Cassy's voice. 'I mean, me and Kyle are okay, he has told me there was nothing going on with him and Alora the other night and we are still going to go to 'The palace' at the weekend, we wouldn't miss it for the world and..'

'It's fine Cass honestly I'm going to work now but if you want to talk ring me later okay when you're sorted.'

Sadie had no intention of giving up the tracker, definitely not now, she could sense something was going to happen she thought as she opened her pregnancy test.

The Palace Two weeks later

The Six bells in the centre of town were filling up before the opening of 'The Palace' night club just a five-minute walk away. The usual middle aged day time day drinker's pub was welcoming a younger generation with young women dressed in sophisticated evening gowns accompanied with young men in suits to comply with the opening's strict dress code for tonight only. The landlord had laid on extra bar staff, hence the unusual long wait at the bar. Four out of the six had arrived and it hadn't been too awkward, they were all adults, and it was *his* round. He wondered why she was so late, he hoped they were both still coming, or rather he hoped *she* would be still coming. At work, they both remained professional, it was all part of the fun, however because she was now late, he realised how much he longed to see her and was curious of how good she may look. His thoughts were abruptly interrupted by an elbow knocking into him to his right with a rowdy group of men that had pushed their way slightly in front of him to be served. 'Sorry mate!' The half-hearted apology came from the larger one of the group. Luckily one of the bar staff came to his rescue who had acknowledged his impatient beer mat tapping, as he was also joined by his partner. 'I'll have a double please, judging by the wait and can you get the other two some drinks, they have just arrived, save them queuing, I'll give you a hand.'

He looked behind him to his left and caught site of her immediately looking more gorgeous than he had ever seen her looking before.

'Wow, just wow,' she stood out in the crowd, and it was obvious to him as nervous as she looked, her eyes were wandering the room for him too.

The beginning of the evening had started a little awkwardly, however the six of them, all appeared to be enjoying themselves at the new sophisticated, elegant venue. The huge V.I.P area upstairs had provided a bird's eye view for the lucky guests on all the evenings opening entertainment from professional cabaret dancers to an upcoming local rapper and then onto an array of sophisticated Moulin Rouge dancers. Ladies of the V.I.P area had all made a huge effort with some wearing extremely stylish ballgowns and evening dresses. There had been rumours of some general ticket holders being turned away upon entry due to the 'requirement of the attire for the evening' not being met. The suits worn by the men had all been tailored and were form fitting and the quality of appearance of the evening of both sexes were attracting an accompanying a graceful and stylish manner. A selection of foods such as Native lobster & Veal sweetbread & Langoustine were among the light buffet offered with vegan options such as Gnocchi and Wild mushrooms as a starter then followed by Tournedos of Beef or Bresse Duck or Guacamole & Mango salad and desserts of Caramel Parfait or Vanilla Mouselline were offered to V.I.P's only while they dined to two live pianists, washed down with expensive red, white, and sparkling champagne. By 11.30pm the dance floor was opened to the sounds of one of London's top DJ's.

The affair

Her

She caught sight of him looking at her from behind in her ink blue silk backless mermaid dress that clung to her body in all the right places in the large exclusive art deco mirror as she danced and noticed how he was slowly but steadily moving closer to her from behind. She had avoided any contact with him all evening until now where she had caught his stare. His shirt jacket was now off along with his tie and the pecks of his muscles were showing under the lights through his crisp shirt.

The DJ threw an old 1980's track that she remembered dancing to at family parties, where people would all sit closely behind each other in rows and use their arms to dance back and forth and side to side whilst remaining sitting down on the floor.

She was the last to be seated as she carefully lifted up her mermaid silk dress for it not to tear. After a while, she felt the grip of the firm muscled legs from behind her, wrapped around her as she suddenly felt his breath on her bare neck and slim back.

Him

He wanted her there and then, to her that was obvious, to him he couldn't hide it and to everyone else's oblivion caused by the loud music and party atmosphere. He felt her silk dress between his legs, and she felt him too. He wanted to rip it over her head as he whispered in her ear.

'I want you and I know you want me to.' It was in that moment that she stood up and walked away.

Him

His eyes darted around the now packed danced floor, he couldn't see her.. He thought she may have just gone to the ladies, but that was a while ago. He had been watching her all night, watching her dance, watching her body in that silk dress. He had almost tasted her perfume when she had felt his breath on her slender neck. He had lost sight of her now but needed to find her. He wanted her and she wanted him.

He pushed through the air of the oblivious atmosphere of cheesy eighties tunes and the arms and legs of 'no one's watching me dancing and I don't care. He pushed past the young couple that were almost blocking the walkway with their obvious argument like they had forgotten where they were, and past the group of young men trying to impress the young women to their left until he had made it down the scarlet red carpeted stairs to the lower level. He searched the lower floor for her for a while until he realised she had left and headed towards the exit.

'You will need your pass if you come back in please.'
He answered the security guy with a nod. He was on a mission to find her. He entered the cool breeze of the outside world and started walking briskly, oblivious to the fact that he was being watched.

Her

*She needed some air, she needed to cool down, she needed a moment. Seriously? In front of everyone, it was way too close for her liking, however that was the problem she **had** liked it. Moments before he had been dancing too close to her friend too, she hadn't liked that, and she hadn't liked the ridiculous feeling of the pang of jealousy that caught her for a moment either. 'Pathetic.' She pushed through the air of the oblivious atmosphere of cheesy eighties tunes and the arms and legs of 'no one's watching me dancing and I don't care. She pushed past the very intimate young couple that were up against the wall so closely like they had almost forgotten where they were, and past the group of young men trying to impress the young women to their left until she had made it down the scarlet red carpeted stairs to the exit.*

'If you want to come back in love, just show your pass please, thank you.' She didn't mean to totally ignore the security guy, she just needed to escape this madness quick. She wanted him tonight and was struggling to hide it and she was struggling to fight it. She entered the cool breeze of the outside world and started walking briskly to the vibration of missed calls oblivious to the fact that she was being followed.

Him

He called her name; she didn't hear him over the noise of cars and taxi's hooting through the busy streets of London, until he had caught up with her and she jumped. 'Sorry.'

He noticed her beauty even more so, glowing under the shimmer of the bright yellow streetlamp, the deafening music from a car that had stopped at the traffic lights now fading as it drove off. In that moment the two of them were oblivious to the city street. She shuddered at his touch as he stroked her arm as he moved closer. 'Not here.' He took off his suit jacket and wrapped it around her shoulders she felt the touch of his hand resting gently on her bottom over her silk fish tail dress as he guided her and she followed, submissively. Five-star hotels stood hugely on almost every street. Still no words were spoken. The revolving door welcomed them as time stood still for a moment. She knew it was wrong, he knew it was wrong, it didn't matter. Her whole body was longing for his touch like a powerful magnetic force. The luxury of the honeymoon suite went unnoticed as he pushed her backwards onto the extra wide bed, lowering himself on top of her, his mouth open as he lifted her dress, teasing her with his warm tongue on her neck while slowly removing her underwear. His tongue travelled slowly over her breasts down past her tummy while she removed his trousers. She let out a moan as her body trembled as his mouth lowered to the top of her open legs as she held the back of his head tightly and pushed herself on to his face. Her orgasm encouraged him impatiently inside her, he couldn't wait any longer and turned her masterfully onto her front lifting off her dress at the same time. He threw off his shirt as he breathed on the back of her neck. Thrusting himself while observing the shape of her bottom, while she reached her second orgasm.

He rolled her on her back and entered her again. Once he was inside her she knew she had a hold over him and she used it shamelessly as she squealed with delight at the sexiness of his manly chest as he held the back of her hair with the correct amount of force and passion. His experienced hands wandering all over her body as if she was being touched by more than one of him. Their mouths caressing while he slowly motioned his body as she held on to the firmness of his thighs then onto his buttocks. Her screams were uncontrollable as he held her hand over her mouth as she bit the side of it in delight, their bodies intense and simultaneous as she orgasmed for a third time, until he lost control and they collapsed together, still breathing heavily with passion moments after.

It had happened, the built-up sexual tension was now released. There was no going back. They had been watched and followed to the Five-star luxury hotel and it had been noted and their affair would be used as blackmail. Their passion would now be put to the test of its longevity caused by the drama that was about to unfold. Had it been worth it? Only time would tell.

Lust is when you fall for someone's beauty

Love is when you fall for someone's soul

***

Chapter Fourteen

'To answer your question Johnny, yes I forgave Blake eventually, and yes I moved back in with him and he stayed teetotal, and things were good, for a while anyway. Cassy finally forgave Kyle for his 'behaviour' with me as she called it, in my bedroom. As for Sadie and Lucian that's another story but something happened, especially after the night at the opening of 'The Palace' in the West End.

Cassy

Cassy woke up alone, she missed Kyle beside her after a night out, especially, and she missed him cooking her a full English breakfast too. She wondered if she had been too rash in leaving his house and sharing his two-bedroom flat with one of her colleagues. Her head was banging after last night at The Palace and she just wanted one of their Sunday mornings together in bed, like they used to. She decided to message him.

'Morning x'

Kyle

Today Kyle was going to make an effort with Cassy, he

hadn't been treating her right lately and he needed to try and put things right between them. His empty bed made him realise that he had missed her company more than he had thought he would, although he still liked his own time alone, his 'Kyle time.' He showered, had a coffee, and popped out to buy some groceries for breakfast, she loved a full English breakfast after a night out and he decided he would invite her round and cook her one. As he left the supermarket his phone beeped.

'Morning x.'

He put his shopping down against the ATM outside and smiled.

'Morning you, how do you fancy a full English?' x

She sighed happily and replied instantly.

'Yes please see you in half hour xx.'

Alora

Alora was thinking of Blake as soon as she opened her eyes. *'I hope he didn't drink last night.'* She felt slightly responsible if he had. She hadn't heard anything from him since last night and it was almost 11am. She felt guilty and decided to ring him.

Blake

There was a cool breeze blowing yet the sea looked playful. Blake felt a sense of nostalgia as he observed the blue skies above him. He was waiting for Alora who had gone to the ice cream van. Perfect. She had looked lovely last night, stunning he thought proudly. His peaceful thoughts were interrupted suddenly by his phone ringing. He had slept through a few calls including Alora's, however she rang again. Blake awoke to the realisation that he had been dreaming as he noted the missed calls from her. His head was pounding from too much alcohol again. *'What a total dick I have been,'* he thought, *'again.'*

Sadie

Sadie counted to ten, *'1 2 3 4 5 6 7 8 9 and breathe.'* She repeated this over and over again. *'Remember Sadie calm, pretend come on you are a little actress, you can do this you can pretend you are not angry and play the dutiful little wife, you can do it.'* She reassured her reflection in her bathroom hanging mirror. The anger inside her was immense, however she kept to her own promise and reached for her soap bag in her bathroom cabinet and peeled off the wrapper and locked the bathroom door. Two minutes passed.

'Oh my god, oh my god, oh my god! No way two lines.' She could not believe it – Two lines = Pregnant. She needed to another one a.s.a.p. She drank as much water as she could and one hour later there it was again – Two lines = Pregnant.

*

Lucian

Lucian had gone for a run as soon as he had woken, he had needed to clear his head. Last night had been a nightmare, in more ways than one. It was meant to be a great promotion for his business, a chance to bring in more custom and it was going well at first until Sadie had embarrassed him again. She had made him look like a total idiot with her drunken flirting. He hadn't seen her for most of the night and it was *her* that had pushed him into leaving The Palace. He wasn't happy with her this morning; he would have loved to have her support last night. He loved her deeply, but he didn't always like her. He had originally felt guilty last night until he had gone home and discovered that she wasn't there, which was when his own guilt completely vanished. He wanted them to work, he had needed her support, he was already anxious waiting for the D.N.A result.

Sadie checked the tracker; Lucian was on his run in the park as a message came through from Cassy.
    'Sorry about last night.'
    'I bet she is.' Sadie muttered to herself.

Alora accepted Blake's offer of a Sunday roast dinner. She barely had anything in her fridge, and she was drained, mentally and physically. He asked her to drive as he said he 'didn't feel like it,' which Alora guessed that it meant he would have been drinking heavily last night.
    'Lovely, what shall I bring?'

She couldn't be bothered to question him, lecture him or anything today. There had been too many drama's recently and last night had made her realise she just needed peace and quiet, a roast dinner, maybe a dessert and a relax.

Johnny looked into Alora's eyes and held her stare. The corners of his eyes smiling at her while looking into her soul. *'His mum was right,'* she thought those emerald eyes complimenting the emerald isle.

'You don't love him Lor do you? Blake I mean, I can tell, I know you.'

'Hey Johnny, don't be giving me the green-eyed monster look with those emerald eyes haha.'

'Well yeah perhaps there is a bit of that Lor, I'd give anything for a Sunday roast now, but joking aside c'mon you haven't answered my question. You don't love him do you? I know you, better than you think.'

'Honestly Johnny, no I don't think I do. You know at first it was easy, he seemed, I don't know keen, he was keen to make me happy, keen on me, acted like a gentleman..'

'Oh yeah right Lor, he treated you like a princess didn't he, I mean until he had a skinful.'

'I know and that was the problem, on the surface he was cool and calm and very gentlemanly, a hard worker, a great provider, my mum liked him, he had his own business, but…'

'Yeah, there was a great big but Lor, I mean we all like a drink now and then, or we did, jeez I'm Irish we work hard and play hard but it's how it makes you, it's how it affects your behaviour. The guy has issues and drink just accentuates it for him doesn't it, and that's okay if you want to put up with that Lor, but I have seen it with me own eyes from my da, and I wouldn't want you to end up suffering when you could have any pick of who you want in the world, you know that don't you?' Johnny gently stroked Alora's forehead and then slowly led his finger over nose and down to her lips as they held each other's gaze for a moment.

'Well, what about you Johnny, there must have been someone after me?' Alora jumped up from her wall and pushed her face right up to his, just like she used to when they were younger to see if he was telling the truth, she held her stare for a moment.

'If you blink you are lying Johnny.' She said in her child like voice. Johnny burst into a fit of giggles.

'Haha I had forgotten all about that Lor, you make me laugh.'

'Well?'

'How can I not blink with those huge eyes of yours staring into mine.' He realised she was not letting up.

'Okay there *was* someone Lor, a little while after you, her name was Roisin spelt R O I S I N but pronounced Ro-Sheen.

'Did you love her?'

'At one point, yes, yes I did.'

'And what happened, was you still together, you know when you passed?'

'No, we had split before then.'

'Why did you split? You don't mind telling me do you? I mean I have told you my story, well nearly.'

'Nearly?'

'Yeah I know Johnny there is more, be patient, anyway, where did you meet?'

'At a funeral, well a wake.'

'Pah! Sorry Johnny well actually you mean one of your Irish party's that you lot here call a wake!'

'Yeah for sure, I think we had karaoke to be fair too, yeah we did, that's when I first noticed her she had a voice of an angel and then I got up and sang The Fields of Athenry.'

'Oh my god Johnny I remember you all singing that at yours when we were kids, aw you will have to sing that for me sometime, anyway, go on.'

'She played hard to get at first she did, but she stood out ya know, her face was quite angelic, to look at she had quite dark features, big eyes like yours but not quire as almond shaped as yours, her hair was thick and curly like yours too but dark, really dark.'

'And?'

'Well, I asked her out and we had a laugh and had some fun on a few dates and then, well she liked a drink too, but sadly she preferred a drink to everything else. You see in the end, she just kept drinking. At first it was a sneaky drink on lunch then it just got worse and worse, and she got nasty if I tried to help her, she started hiding bottles and I just couldn't do it anymore. Eventually we split and she hooked up with someone else, you see Lor....' Johnny's usually cheery face frowned for a moment, 'you can only help someone so much, they have to want to help themselves, otherwise it won't work, and it will just make you miserable. I did hear that she did, eventually sought the help that she needed, she sorted herself out and met someone else, and I assume she is okay, I know she has a couple of kids now too. So, I am happy for her, but, like I said we all must help ourselves by accepting that we need help in the first place. Just like Blake with you, help him yes, but you are still a young, vivacious, clever, funny, and not to mention in my eyes a beautiful woman and if you go back, you should take some time for you, for Alora, find out what you really want. 'Johnny, you do talk some sense.' Alora said as she shed a tear.

'Hey, I'm losing you I know I am, you have just shed a tear, which means it won't be long until you are back, you are getting better, come here. We need to sing before you go. Come on let's go to the hill, but the hill here in Ireland, I will show you my hill, where I used to think of you all the time.'

Alora's face lit up. 'On one condition? We sing The Fields of Athenry on the way!'

'Deal come on.'

'My lonely prison wall, I heard a young girl calling....'

'Aw listen, can you hear your granny, she's singing The Fields of Athenry with us Johnny.'

The Park bench looked inviting for Lucian as he decided he needed to stop for a breather after his 5km run. He checked his running time as he took a few sips of water. It was faster than usual he noted as his phone pinged a notification, which took him to his social media account, reminding him that there were lots of pictures taken last night at 'The Palace.'

'You are kidding me. Look at the state of her, my god, lovely picture Sadie, photo bombing my picture of me and the CEO of a multinational company shaking hands on a serious business deal. Thanks Sadie for flashing your tits behind us, eight laughing faces already, great. Oh no and there's more, bloody hell Sadie, a picture of you throwing up outside the club as well. That must have been when you disappeared for a while. Brilliant, great for my business Sadie!'

'Hi Cassy, how's you this morning? Yes I'm sorry too. Look can you come in earlier in the morning please, so we can chat? Thanks.' Lucian sighed.

Sadie's discovery this morning had totally distracted her for a moment, two pregnancy tests had confirmed it and any anger or suspicion she held for Lucian at this moment in time had been totally diminished. She was delighted. She didn't want to tell anyone just yet, plus at some point this week the letter should arrive regarding Lucian's D.N.A result. A wave of nausea came over her and she headed straight back to the bathroom.

Alora felt nervous, like she was on a first date again. Maybe this was a new beginning she wondered. She liked the idea of starting all over again and had even made a little more effort with her hair and a few sprays of her 'expensive special occasion' favourite perfume. She still had mixed emotions as last night had not gone completely to plan, however today was a fresh start, so with her strawberry cheesecake in hand, Blake's favourite, she knocked on his door.

Alora assumed Blake would ask her why she had knocked the door, he never did. She never used to knock, she had her own key and was tempted to walk straight in. He answered the door like he was accepting a parcel delivery, his face pale and non expressionless. Alora knew instantly that he had drunk last night, and the scent of a mixture of stale beer and mint confirmed it as he welcomed her in.

'How are you?' Blake asked as he glanced at the strawberry cheesecake.

'A little tired, after last night, but okay, you?' Alora already knew the answer, he looked like he was carrying the weight of the world on his shoulders without even trying to hide it.

'I'm okay.' He lied. Alora felt guilty, his house was a bit of a mess, which was unlike Blake, usually his house was spotless, he could spend an hour cleaning his bathroom.

Blake gestured towards the sofa. 'Cuppa?'

Alora took off her coat as she sat down, then got back up to hang it up in the hallway, Blake was usually extremely fussy about everything being in its place, however, today he appeared to have no bother about him at all.

'Yes please.'

Blake was just about holding it together, as he run the tap for another glass of water, to sound of the boiling kettle. He had wanted to make such an effort today, he had missed Alora but now she was here, he barely had the energy to walk to the kitchen, he didn't feel great, and this hangover was the worst one yet.

'You don't mind if we get a takeaway instead do you Alora? I'm struggling.' Alora admired his admission. It was honest at least. It was a start.

'That tasted lush, thank you.'

'Wow you were hungry; you have got some appetite Cass.' Kyle teased.

For the rest of the day the two of them enjoyed a 'Sofa Sunday' as Cassy liked to call it. A day of watching a couple of films, eating rubbish, the odd glass of wine perhaps then maybe later some fun in the bedroom, however there was no urge or need for sex today from either of them, each other's company was enough, Cassy thought happily as she lay with her head on Kyle's chest. She had barely seen her phone today as well, which was a first for Cassy as Kyle at one point mentioned. It was only when Kyle took a shower that Cassy caught up with her messages and some of her social media.

'No fucking way!'

Lucian went straight up to the bedroom when he returned home after his run, he was fuming. He had wanted to mention the pictures and the state of Sadie last night. She never took his business seriously and he had a lot riding on the opening of The Palace last night. As he opened the door she lay there fast asleep. He sighed with annoyance and then jumped in the shower. It would have to wait until later.

Monday morning

A nervous Cassy arrived at work forty-five minutes early as per Lucian's request, even though thirty minutes would have sufficed. Katrina the office gossip/receptionist welcomed her with a 'Morning?' As to why are you here so early kind of 'Morning.' Cassy was polite but totally ignored her leading 'Morning?' question.

Lucian was running late, and the Monday morning traffic had been diverted. He was annoyed at himself and decided to call Cassy and apologise. Saturday night was not discussed at all, to Cassy's amazement.

'Sorry Cassy, thanks for going into work early, I am stuck in a diversion and then I have an out of office meeting at 10am, so I may as well go straight there now. So, I was, originally going to ask you to join me and Mia on this midweek business trip to Germany that Mia has organised, but...anyway......well, it's just us two going now, as I needed someone to hold the fort here and I forgot that Luke was off this week. So, if I could put you in charge please? It is a massive opportunity for the company and I want to view some cars myself and close a deal I have been working on so, it means I would need you to be in work every day this week, without taking any holiday or time off. We will be flying out Wednesday then back on Sunday. This week is appearing to be quite busy, aside from the usual meetings. Six of the vehicles are in for an M.O.T and Service, the list of vehicles is on my desk, actually if you could double check that for me please?'

Cassy was grateful that Lucian could not see the look of disappointment on her face as she searched through the list on Lucian's desk, she had been looking forward to going to Germany.

'Found it.' She managed.

'Great, anyway I need them booking in with Blake at the garage so, they will need to be taken there individually. So that is it apart from a few loose ends that I am going to try and sort in the next couple of days, but any problems just call me, is that okay? Obviously I will pay you extra, I need to sort that with payroll.'

'Yes of course.' She managed to sound more positive than she felt.

Sadie had listened in on the call, *'Who the hell is Mia? What does he mean he was going to take me? Just the two of them I don't think so!'* Sadie's exhilaration regarding her planned pregnancy was dismissed for a while. Her morning sickness was delaying her arrival for work, and now she was fuming at Lucian's plans to go away with another woman. She needed to act fast.

Alora declined Kyle's offer of a car share again and decided it would be 'for the best' if they both made their own way to work. She also had stayed at Blake's last night as he had seemed really low yesterday and she had felt partly to blame. She'd had a very relaxing day on his sofa yesterday while he had slept, a lot. There had been very little communication between the two of them, but she felt that she needed to look after him for a while, the promotion could wait, she needed to concentrate on herself and Blake.

 'Hi Mia

Hope you're good, it looks like just me and you are going on the business trip, Sadie can't make it and Cassy is busy. So just the one room for me please, can you just send me the flight link thank you 😊

Regards
Lucian.

'Woo ooh! That has brightened up a dull Monday morning, I get to go on an all-expenses paid business trip with the drop dead blue-eyed gorgeous businessman called Lucian 😊'

Regards
Mia.

The affair

They had been watched, followed to the Five-star luxury 'Royale hotel' and it had been noted and their affair would be used as blackmail. Their passion would now be put to the test of its longevity caused by the drama that was about to unfold. Had it been worth it?

Her and Him

Again, they had remained professional at work on Monday, however they both individually, in their own quiet moment of the day reflected back to Saturday night.

Her

It wasn't even the morning after the night before, it was minutes and the heat of his body, and the warmth of the hotel room, which made her want to jump into the shower as soon as she could.

Him

'This could either go two ways,' he thought as he opened his eyes. 'She could either say this was a huge mistake or we would do it all over again,' he thought as he watched her enter the shower. He was hoping it would be the latter.

Her

She showered thoroughly cleaning away the guilt from her actions. She stepped out of the shower, sat on the edge of the bed, and noted the look in his eye.

'Right, I've been thinking, we need to talk about us, me, and you, I think I will tell him later and you can tell her.'

Him

He shot straight up off the bed and wrapped a towel around him and flicked on the terribly slow boiling kettle, urging it to boil faster, as if the sound of it would give him more time to respond and hide his shocked silence. 'What? No, no and bloody no, are you for real?' Were his immediate thoughts. Instead with his back to her still, he suggested. 'Coffee?'

He felt her eyes follow the line of his clenched jaw; it wasn't easy hiding his anxiousness at her ridiculous suggestion, and they both knew it in that moment of awkwardness.

Her

'Yes please, one sugar and milk thanks.' Her voice quavered as she sighed heavily and ran a hand through her hair, as she sat on the bed, she observed his silence as he past her a coffee.

'You haven't answered me, we need to talk about what has just happened you know, it changes everything.'

Him

'Does it? What is it with you women and talking? I mean we have just had fantastic sex and you want to talk?' He had to bite his tongue hard to refrain from speaking his true thoughts and instead sat next to her on the bed, he hunched forward to avoid any eye contact and fiddled with a loose thread on the bed cover.

'Look, it was lovely, but do you not think the others will be wondering where we both are?' He waved his phone to show her a missed call. I her moment of passion, she hadn't given the others much thought.

'Yes you are right we need to get back, make up some story I don't know, we will think on the way back.'

'Well, I am going to go home now, don't you think you should do the same, or you go home, and I will go back to The Palace, which would make more sense, and we will talk later? Please don't do anything hasty, this was lovely, but..' She shows a quick smile, however she is equally saddened and confused and he notices her expression

'I promise we will talk later, but let's keep this hush between us, you are lovely, and we have something and it's fun it really is.' He was digging a whole deeper and deeper and he knew it, her facial expression changed, and she snapped and threw her dress back on.
Her

'Yeah you right we had a bit of fun, because we were both being neglected and now you have had your fun with me you can toss me aside and we will say no more!'

Before he could reply her phone rang and she answered it without thinking. The noise of The Palace nightclub was echoing in the background along with the caller's shout. *'ARE YOU OKAY? WHERE ARE YOU? I THOUGHT YOU HAD GONE HOME?'*

'I AM GOING HOME! I MEAN.. I AM AT HOME.'

'AS LONG AS YOU ARE OKAY?'

'YES FINE YOU JUST ENJOY YOURSELF.'

'OKAY BYE.'
Him

'He picked up his phone, the reality of what had happened tonight had just hit home and had played on his

guilt. 'Hey you ok? Are you still at the club I left for some air? X' **Sent.** He needed to cover his tracks.

Her

She tidied her hair and collected her things together. She balanced onto one foot while sliding her shoe onto the other. The silence in the hotel room between them was now deafening until she spoke.

'I'll go and wait at the taxi rank over the road you just go back to the club, I am going home.' He smiled at her and at that moment she wondered why someone with such a lovely smile could be such a shit.

Him

He felt like a such a shit, he really did as he checked out of the hotel. He watched her get into the taxi safely, it was the least he could do. The city lights were dimming, the liveliness of the London's nightlife was quieting down and the air was now cooler. He looked at his watch It was 2.06am, he thought it would be later than that, he knew he had left the club around 12.30am. He walked at an easy pace back to the club. He needed the walk, he needed to clear his head. He had made a massive mistake, he knew that already, his lust and high sex drive had taken over any rationale. The guilt started to set in. Tonight, was a blip, he needed to put his energy back in to his relationship. He just hoped that this one night would remain a secret between them.

Her

The taxi ride home was solemn, she could not be doing with the small talk from the taxi driver which her stunned silence showed. Tears started rolling down her cheeks.

In the height of passion, the two of them had been oblivious to that fact that their secret was no longer just between them, as they would soon find out.

Monday continued…

Her

Still nothing from him, no flirting, no apology, no mention of them two in bed together Saturday night. They had to communicate regarding business and work and that was it. It was a mixture of emotions, however she needed to concentrate on her own relationship, it needed fixing and so did his. Still, she missed the excitement.

Him

*He remained professional at work, he had to, he had no choice. He wasn't going back there again ever. He had made one big mistake and he knew it. Onwards and upwards was his motto and he would put it all behind him. Hopefully they could **both** put it behind them, he thought optimistically.*

Her

A notification of a text message interrupted her thoughts. 'I know about your secret little love affair. I will keep quiet on one condition, to find out what it is meet me at the Globe at 6pm.' She felt sick.

'Who is this?'

'Meet me at 6pm and you will find out.'

What choice did she have?

The Globe was a new restaurant in the centre of London that offered so many different cuisines from all around the globe, hence the name. It had private booths inside, but there were some benches outside the front, and a takeaway bar where school children and students spent time together after school.

On her arrival she decided to purchase a coffee and observe her 'blackmailer' from the takeaway bar outside where she let her mind work overtime, at one point she thought it may be him playing some sick joke. Or, it could be her partner, tricking her into turning up which would make her look guilty. She wondered who the blackmailer could be, and a number of people sprung to mind. She thought back to Saturday night, the walk to the hotel, they had both been a little too brazen, both missing from the Palace at the same time and for a couple of hours. She had been surprised on Sunday morning that no questions had been asked, although she had been in such a sorry state, she hadn't really thought about it at the time.

She pulled up her hood and wrapped a scarf around her face and put on her dark sunglasses although it was still fairly mild, even though it was now towards the end of summer. It was too late. She almost dropped her coffee over the table in shock as her blackmailer casually joined her.

'Ah, this seems more private here than the Globe, I will grab a coffee and then we can talk.'

Her

'Wow, you really have some nerve don't you. Who do you think you are?' She wanted to say to her blackmailer, however she took an inward sigh, gritted her teeth and listened instead.

'Now we all know that if your other half found out about your little rendezvous then your relationship would be over, correct?'

'I have no idea what you are talking about.' She lied with a sigh of annoyance.

'So, these pictures I have here on my phone, won't go anywhere, if you help me that is, and if you can, then I will delete all these pictures in front of you, when you have completed the task okay?' Her heart sank as she realised they really had been caught, judging by the photos of them.

'What task?' She swallowed nervously.

'I will get to that in a moment, first we have some conditions, okay, you keep this between me and you only, okay?'

She paused for a moment to try and contain her anger, she felt that any minute now she could really lose her shit, eventually and reluctantly she agreed. 'Okay.'

'Okay I have some questions and, I want honest answers. 'I take it you are still seeing him.'

'No.'

'I said honest answers.'

'I said NO.' This time she couldn't hide her anger.

'Okay well whatever, the thing is, he must never know about our meeting, ever ok?'

'Depends.' She felt brave as her anger took control, her fists clenched tighter and tighter.

The blackmailer scrolled down to a picture and flashed the phone in front of her. It *was* a photo of him and her outside the Royale hotel.

Her face went as pale as her fists, and she loosened her grip. 'Okay I won't tell *him* about this blackmail, but you do know blackmailing is a criminal offence?' The bluff was called, she tried anyway.

'And so is adultery.'

There was no comment for a while, just a pause from an unknowingly friendly waitress. 'Did you want anything else?' She hadn't been able to eat since she had received the anonymous blackmail message this morning. The blackmailer however with little conscious and clearly no regret felt hungry.

'Yes another coffee and one of your doughnuts please? Thank you.'

'Okay so now we have that sorted, where were we? Oh yes right, we have confirmed this little meeting is between me and you so now I will tell you what I need you to do for me okay?'

'Go on.'

Chapter Fifteen

Johnny sat on the wall alone for a couple of minutes. Alora had disappeared for a while, and he knew his time was running out with her. He was pleased she was getting better, but, he had one thing to do, and he wanted Alora to go back to a different life. He wanted the best for her and in his eyes he knew whatever happened Blake was no good for her, he owed it to her, and he thought the world of her, her happiness to him was everything. Alora appeared as quickly as she left, and Johnny held her gaze for a while. 'What?'

'Here you are, oh nothing I was just in deep thought as you were gone a bit longer this time Lor, come on continue with your story before I lose you for good.'

'I saw my mum; Johnny I saw her face.'

'That's great sweetheart, how was she? Better than you I should imagine.'

Alora giggled, 'stop it Johnny, don't make me laugh. She was happy, smiling at me as I opened my eyes, I felt her hand on my face, she was kind of blurry at first, but then I managed a smile at her, and she burst into tears.'

Alora frowned and Johnny put his arm around her.

'Eh come on you stop thinking, I told you it's not good,

why the sad face Lor? Come on you are clearly on your way back to life, you lucky bitch ya,' he soothed as Alora laid her head on his chest. 'I know Johnny, I'm just scared, my life was a mess before all this, and now being here with you I'm in two minds as to whether I want to go back yet or not. I miss my job, my mum, dad, brother and nieces and nephews, some of my friends, but the drama the mess, even Blake I don't miss that anymore. I don't miss him.'

'Well, that's good, isn't it you can soon change that, the drama, Blake and his mess, that's up to you sweetheart.' He soothed as he stroked her hair.

'What about you though Johnny, us, me and you?'

'I know Lor, I'm loving this time together, but ya know, what will be will be and well when your time is up I'll be here, I'm not going anywhere, I'll be waiting, you know that ready to belt out The Fields of Athenry. Look you cannot change fate, but I will tell you now Lor, from the bottom of my heart. I love you more than life itself and I always will, and for whatever reason, it has bought us together, it will all be alright in the end I promise ya. Why don't you spend some time with your Aunt Ede later for a bit, I have hogged you since you've been here and there's loads to see, but first finish off your story before it's too late.'

'Yeah I suppose you are right Johnny..'

'I'm always right you know it.'

'Ha, where was I? Well, it was the Monday evening after the drama at The Palace…'

Sadie was fuming, Lucian is going to get an earful when he gets home, *'Mia? Who is she? I know there was some blonde hanging around him, Saturday night,'* she recalled, *'I thought she said her name was Michelle though. She probably flirted with him, when I was out of sight for a while, my own stupid fault.'*

'Hiya love!' Lucian sounded far too happy, which added to Sadie's fury. She totally ignored him until he entered the kitchen. She was chopping vegetables furiously. Lucian noticed her anger as she glanced sideways at him.

'Good day?' He tried.

'Busy, you? Was her curt response.

'Yes, productive.'

'I bet.'

'Okay come on Sadie spit it out.'

'What?' Sadie was biting her tongue like she never had before. How the hell could she let on that she knew about his business trip and that he wasn't taking her? She couldn't tell him about her tracker on him. She had to think quickly.

'Sorry,' she sighed, she backtracked she would change her approach. 'I have just had a really shitty day and..'

'Clients?' Lucian interrupted, slightly relieved, he was planning on her being in a good mood so he could go on this business trip with Mia, with no drama, he wasn't even going to mention them awful pictures on social media.

'Yes, talking of which,' Sadie thought on the spot very quickly. 'What are you doing Thursday?' Shannon needs a male model for a massage?'

'Ah, Thursday, well Sadie you know I mentioned this business trip to Germany..'

'You mentioned it once, a few weeks ago, yes.'

'Erm I mentioned it a few times, and again at the meal on Saturday at The Palace and..'

'Oh yeah Cassy was on about it, she invited me I remember now.' Sadie lied and added a high pitch to her tone as if she assumed that she was invited.

'Well, no Cassy isn't going.'

'Oh, really why not? Just me and you then when is it?'

'Well yeah you could come but..'

'When is it Lucian?' Sadie didn't mean to sound like a headmistress who was trying to discipline a child in her office, but she did.

'Wednesday until Sunday?' Lucian's voice quietened.

'That's fine I can arrange my appointments,' Sadie's voice was now back up to the higher positive tone.

Lucian's face dropped; he didn't hide it either.

'What's up Lucian, don't you want me there? It will be nice just me and you and..'

'It's a business trip Sadie.'

'I know that don't worry; I can go shopping while you do all your boring stuff.' Sadie suggested. *'Come on Lucian spill, tell me about Mia!'* It was as if he read her thoughts.

'Thing is it will be the three of us, me, you and Mia. You met her Saturday night, she works for..'

'Who?' Sadie interrupted, 'Mia, the blonde tall one botoxed lips that one? Yeah that's fine Lucian tell her to book my flight too.' Sadie's voice slightly lowered when she realised what she had just said.

'*Hang on how did she know Mia was booking our flights?*' Lucian thought suspiciously.

'Crafty bitch that Sadie one, so what happened did he take her Lor?' Johnny asked curiously.

'Nope she messed that up, aw there's a butterfly look it's beautiful.' Alora loved butterflies and she was able to get really close to it and its beautiful array of colours.

'Where was I? Oh yes Sadie, she even tried to tell Lucian she was pregnant and that didn't stop him going, but he got on that plane with Mia on that Wednesday and, whatever happened in Germany, none of us know but Lucian was furious with Sadie, that I do know.

'Good, about time that Lucian one stood up to her and the D.N.A test?'

'That came back that Lucian was not the father to Louie.'

'Oh right, so what about you and boring Blake?'

'Johnny!'

'Sorry only joking. Come on you and Blake what happened between you giving him a second chance? Don't tell me you were all okay until Lucian and that Sadie one got back together and threw yet another fucking dinner party and it all went tit's up again?'

'Well, pretty much.'

'Fuck off! Haha no way!'

'Johnny!' Johnny... Johnny? Alora called as he disappeared for a few seconds.

'Where did you go?'

'Sorry Lor, I'm back now and haha, honestly it's just the way you were explaining. I can't wait to hear of dinner party number three, but I can't take much more at the minute. Go and see your Aunt Ede for a bit and we will resume.' Johnny's cheeky laugh slowly faded until he was out of Alora's sight.

Aunt Ede was happily chatting away at what Alora called the halfway house, she loved a chat and there appeared to be one of Aunt Ede's old friends called Barbara that had now joined them. Aunt Ede and Barbara used to go ballroom dancing together and that is where Barbara had met her second husband Dennis, who had now joined them too. 'Hello dear, how are you, you remember my great niece Alora don't you Barb?'

'Oh yes, hello sweetheart, I'd say good to see you, but I am assuming you won't be here for long hopefully, do you remember Dennis my husband, he's finally joined us, I just had a moan at him for being a bit late didn't I love.' Aunt Ede and Alora both shared a giggle.'

'Yes you did Barb nothing changes, she loves to have a moan does our Barb, I was just catching up with a few old mates and to be fair there is more here than I thought there would be.' Dennis the smartly dressed elderly man said dryly as he put his arm around his wife. 'Anyway, let's go and have a mingle Dennis leave Alora and Ede to it, leave your stick you won't need that here will you?' Barbara bossed to Alora's amusement as Aunt Ede gave Alora a huge hug, 'come on then pet what have you been up to, tell me all about it.'

Chapter Four

Present One day after the accident.

'Cassy arrested really?'

'Well, she was taken into the police station.'

'No way. I wonder what's happened?'

'I don't know but Lucian came to work early he was here before me and that Sadie one has come in all bleary eyed even though she was trying to cover it in makeup, she looks like she has been crying…'

'Oh, really wow, find out what you can, wish I hadn't taken a day's holiday now.'

'I bet, that's a point, I hope we will get paid for this afternoon, I mean I'd rather stay here and find out what's going on to be honest, but I will, you know me I have got my contacts. Ooh I think Lucian's coming gotta go bye..' Katrina, Lucian's receptionist whispered quicky to her colleague as she hung up as Lucian approached her looking tired, fed up and a little dishevelled.

'Katrina, can you ..erm please notify everyone that they have the afternoon off as of now please, full pay, thank you, I am closing for the afternoon.'

'Yes, no problem I will do it now.' Katrina acted very

professional as usual; she didn't ask any questions and she hid the fact that she was the firm's biggest gossip very well from Lucian. She texted her colleague within seconds. *'Really do you think I will be able to claim my days holiday back?'* Was her colleagues reply.

Cassy looked around the dusty cold interview room cautiously, she made a mental note to stay calm. Jenkins sat in front of her with a 'know it all' look in her eye. There was a young policeman sitting next to Jenkins this time, she wondered where the other guy Wilson was, he seemed okay, she didn't like this Jenkins one.

'So, Cassy,' Jenkins paused for a moment, 'we just wanted to ask you again, as I go over your statement if you did or did not see Alora yesterday, prior to her accident?'

'No, I didn't, I last saw her on Saturday at Lucian and Sadie's house like I told you last night.' Cassy was aware her tone was a little sarcastic, but it was meant to be. Jenkins paused for a moment, took off her glasses and wiped them clean before replying.

'Only we have a witness that has come forward telling us that you and Alora were seen together at around 5.20pm, on Courtyard Road Car Park at the entrance to the park. Could you explain that to us please?'

'What? I wonder who that was!' Cassy thought to herself.

'Well?' Is this correct?' Jenkins urged Cassy to reply.

'No, I didn't see Alora yesterday not at all, not until the hospital like I told you.' Cassy was visibly shaking, and this was noted by Jenkins. Cassy was unsure, yesterday had been a bit of a blur, she was attending a promotion for Lucian at a corporate event at a nearby hotel and had been so nervous she had been drinking at the free bar before her speech. She hadn't eaten a thing and daytime drinking never agreed with her. She couldn't remember much after the event apart from waking up on a bench in the park near Courtyard Road Car Park, very near to where this witness had supposedly seen her with Alora, she tried her best but could not recall her movements. Jenkins sensed her hesitation and persisted.

'Cassy as you know Alora is in a coma and this could quite possibly turn into a murder investigation, so therefore I will ask you again. Did you see Alora at any time yesterday, prior to the accident at your visit to the hospital last night?'

'No, I do not recall seeing Alora at all yesterday prior to visiting her at the hospital last night.'
Jenkins eventually terminated the interview.

'We will be in touch Cassy.'

'Kyle answer the phone you dick.' Cassy muttered to herself as she entered the sunny street on her exit from the police station. Cassy and Kyle hadn't spoken for a few days since the night of the barbeque, but she needed to speak to him quick, she had had a vague flash back of seeing Alora prior to the accident, but she genuinely couldn't remember and now she was panicking.

Kyle pulled his baseball cap down a little more, it was a warm day, but he wanted to be left alone. He needed to be left alone. He didn't want to be found or at least recognised today. He noticed a few missed calls from *Cassy*, he didn't want to speak to her, it was probably something trivial anyway, but he still didn't want anything to do with her after recent events. He at least had had the decency to take the day off work after what had happened to Alora, he thought bitterly as he kicked a coke can from his path to its side. He couldn't take his mind off her. He found himself sitting on the horse jump by the woods and reminisced of happier times, when they had all enjoyed a game of rounders and a picnic right here, in front of the woods. *'My favourite place of the abbey, the sun trap.'* Alora had once said, he couldn't stop thinking about her. His heart sank he did not like this feeling in his heart, and he desperately wanted to see her.

Cassy's phone had completely died.
'Oh great!'
She had tried to flag a cab down at the end of road behind the police station with no joy. It would be quicker to walk home than in the direction of the town centre to the local taxi rank she decided. She eventually came to the park that she had stumbled through yesterday a little worse for wear and sat down on the same bench to take a breath and have a sip of water. After a couple of minutes and after swapping pleasantries with a passer-by dog walker and her cute little King Charles Spaniel, memories of yesterday started to re appear.

Blake gathered some of Alora's belongings from her Toulouse style silver dressing table, her hairbrush lay their neatly along with her pink spotted make up bag, she would hate to wake up to messy hair. She barely wore makeup, only maybe a soft peach coloured lipstick and some mascara on a night out, and she always liked to brush her cheeks with this huge brush that lay their next to the make-up bag Blake reflected, however, she brushed her natural golden hair regularly and always before bedtime, he recalled.

He picked up the silver photo frame that stood to the right of her makeup bag with the picture of himself and Alora and sat back on Alora's bed and stared at it for a moment. It had been there for a couple of years on the dressing table, he hadn't paid that much attention to it previously, but now he had. He noticed Alora's beaming beautiful smile looking out from the picture, she was cuddling a pink teddy bear and Blake was holding her closely from behind her at the side of the pier. A passer by had taken their picture and Alora had been wearing her favourite cotton white jeans and a pretty loose white top that had butterfly shapes on, she loved butterflies. It had been a lovely day at the coast for them both, they had not long been together, only a couple of months, in mid-July and just one week after Sadie and Lucian's first dinner party, it had been a lovely short break and had just been the two of them, in which Blake had been secretly pleased about.

Blake's thoughts were interrupted by his mobile ringing he thought it maybe the hospital, however it was a call from work. Blake had asked his employee 'Jack' to 'hold the fort' for the next couple of days, after what had happened to Alora. He rarely had a day off but now, his business meant nothing.

'Yes Jack?' Blake was slightly annoyed and answered abruptly.

'Hi mate, erm yeah sorry to bother you.. it's just that Mr. Cooper is here again, he's not happy and won't leave until you see him, I wasn't sure what to say I did tell him that…'

'Please tell Mr. Cooper Jack, that I have an emergency and like I told him last week we are waiting for parts, end of. He will have a long wait; I have to go now.. is everything ok otherwise?'

'Yes mate all fine sorry to disturb you.. any news on Alora?'

'Still the same mate no change, I'm going up there now.'

Blake finished packing Alora's belongings and headed to the hospital. He picked up his mobile and saw a message from her, which he ignored, again.

Cassy noticed the jogger running towards her past the bench, and realisation that it was Lucian sent her emotions totally out of control.

'Lucian!'

Kyle had had enough of his own thoughts, he needed to see Alora he needed to be near her, so he headed straight to the hospital and drove around the car park until he found one. Suddenly he spotted what looked very much like Blake's car and inside, sitting next to him in the passenger seat was Sadie. *'Well if Sadie is allowed to go to see Alora with them, then so should I.'*

'As much as I'm loving it here Johnny, I am ready to go and have a look back home and see what is going on, will you come with me please?'

'Course I will, where do you want to go?'

'Firstly to the hospital I want to see who is visiting me.'

'Out of all the places in the world you want to see yourself laying in hospital?'

'Yep.'

'You are crackers girl.'

'I want to try and get some clues, I am ready to face it, someone hit me and I suppose it could have been an accident, but it may not have been, plus when I go back I don't want to be pulled in by Blake again, I want to see things, things that will make my mind up to stay away from him, does that make sense?'

'No, it doesn't at all ya mentalist haha, seriously Lor just don't go back to him end of you deserve better darling.'

'I know but I need to do this Johnny.' Alora said as she tilted her head and waited for his response.

'You don't have to give me those puppy dog eyes you know, I will do whatever you want, but just remember the old saying 'curiosity killed the cat.'

'I wonder if they have let Cassy out yet?' Blake asked.

'God knows, we are not speaking at the moment, so I have no idea and I tried ringing Lucian but he's not answering or when he does he's just being vague again, I have the feeling he is keeping something from me Blake.' Sadie confided.

'Hey, do you remember the last you we were in the back of a car together?' Johnny giggled.

'Shush Johnny they might hear us.'

'They can't haha I'm telling you, but I'll shut up so we can listen.'

'Oh, look there's Kyle aw he must be visiting me.'

'Like what?' Blake asked to an nonresponding Sadie, she didn't know the answer to that, but she would do her best to find out.

'I don't know, but he's hiding something, I have just tracked him, and he is showing as in the park, but he has been stationary for thirty-five minutes.'

'Oh Sade, not that again, I thought them days of tracking him were over, plus he probably is just resting at a bench.'

'What for thirty-five minutes?'

'Maybe, yeah and have you told him that you are here, in this car with me at the hospital?'

'Well, no that's not the point, he's barely speaking to me, so it's different, anyway you'd better go in. I'll wait here for a bit.' Sadie added nodding at the busy car park.

'Honestly nothing changes Sadie tracking Lucian and being all sneaky, I wonder what she is doing with Blake anyway, I want to stay here for a bit and see what Sadie does, or see if she rings anyone, I assume Blake's going in to see me on his own.'

'No shit sherlock.'

'Johnny shush,' Alora laughed, 'I am trying to see what Sadie is typing.'

'She's on her tracker by the looks of it..'

'Oh, there's my mum and dad look!'

'So it is, you mum looks well, your dads aged a bit since I last saw him mind.'

He took a deep breath as he entered the corridor, he hated hospitals he always had, but he needed to see Alora. A lady passed him with her foot in a cast being pushed in a wheelchair, *why couldn't that be Alora? A broken leg would have been easier to deal with, he thought as he* applied gel to his hands. The young nurse gave him a nod of approval as he approached the nurse's station, he nodded back and felt a moments relief of assuming there was no change. An older nurse greeted him and mentioned that her eyes had flickered for a few seconds earlier, this being a common occurrence with patients that were in a coma. Her heart rate had raced a little, other than she was pretty much the same. He thought how pretty and peaceful she looked as he held her hand, almost smiling to himself as he reached for her pillow...

'What the hell do you think you are doing!'

'Michael stop please let go of him please!'

'He just had the pillow over Alora's face Jenny!' He is bloody mental not me; he is lucky I don't do the same to him right here right now, call the police go on while I am holding him quick!'

'I was trying to make her more comfortable; I was putting the pillow behind her head she..'

'No you wasn't you pissing lying bastard!'

'What is going on?' The young nurse came rushing into Alora's room in a panic. Alora's father lost his grip and accidently let him go past him, his wife, and the nurse.

'He had a pillow over Alora's head for Christ's sake you need to call the police!'

'Well, she's not doing a lot is she Sadie other than sit on her phone.'

'No just tracking Lucian as per, he's at the park by the hill where we use to go judging by her phone.'

'Why don't we go there see if we can see what this Lucian one is doing, come on let's go you don't want to be sitting around the hospital do you, you'll be spending enough time when you go back.'

'Yeah you're right Johnny, I don't want to be around Sadie or Blake, and do you know what I don't really want to know, I will have all that to face when I go back, if I go back, it was good to see my mum and dad again though.'

There was no sign of Lucian at the park and Alora was glad. Her and Johnny rolled down the hill like a pair of children, they laughed as they pushed one another, only this time again, there were no cuts or grazes.

Chapter Sixteen

Previously

'It's a girl! Congratulations she's beautiful.'

'Thank you.'

Lucian's heart melted, right there and then. He kissed Sadie on the forehead. 'Well done love,' he said proudly.

'Baby Amelia born today 6.42am 6lb 7 oz.
Mum and baby are doing well, thank you to you all for your wishes.'

'Aw, she's early, she wasn't due for another month, she looks like Lucian.'

'How can you tell that, she's a newborn and I can't see it myself, anyway that's if Lucian *is* the father.'

'Why do you keep insinuating that?'

'Well, they split up for a few months remember?'

'Oh, come on Sadie's not my favourite person but how cute, I'll get them a card and present and arrange to go round.'

Sadie looked down with pure admiration at her little bundle of joy and gently stroked her face. 'Just me, you and daddy now, we are complete Amelia.'

Cassy was both nervous and excited as she unwrapped her birthday present from Kyle. 'Happy Birthday Cass.'

'Wow, thank you Kyle, mwah.' The open envelope revealed two tickets to see her favourite band 'The Tickers,' playing locally in London at The Stadium in December, 'I'm so excited and that was so thoughtful.'

'You're welcome, enjoy your day, I got to dash, Alora's driving, and we have a new teacher starting so going in slightly early today.'

Alora was running unusually late this morning, she opened the curtain and spotted Kyle's car outside.

'Morning, you okay?'

'Morning, yes thanks, just woke up too early this morning, then fell back to sleep, sorry to keep you waiting, did you give Cassy the card and the wine?'

'Yeah she said thanks,'

'What did you get her?'

'Two tickets to see The Tickers, playing at the palace, she loves them.'

'Oh, I think Blake mentioned that he wants to go, he said Sadie booked it for Lucian for his birthday.'

'Oh right, I suppose they will need a night out after all of them night feeds eh, it's not until Christmas though.'

'Yeah talking of which how's Louie?'

'Aw he's great thanks, sixteen months old now, into

everything, including Cassy's make up.'

'Oh dear haha, not her favourite lipstick?'

'Yep exactly that, back was turned for a minute, well she was meant to be watching him while I was in the kitchen, but she was on her phone and he had grabbed her handbag, we had him to stay over Saturday night then most of Sunday, Lisa had a date.'

'Ha, did Cassy like having him over?'

'I don't think she's even keen on kids, I don't even know if she wants to have any herself to be honest, she doesn't even like them.'

'No, I know what you mean, she wasn't keen on the children here at Boadfield primary either haha.'

'Ooh looks like this could be the new teacher, she looks young, but very glamourous.'

'Oh yeah,' Alora parks up and turns the engine off as they arrive at the school and turns to Kyle, 'how is Lisa anyway?'

'Yes she's okay thanks, like I said she had a date Saturday night, she said it went okay, she's enjoying motherhood actually, it seems to have sorted her out a bit, she still swears that Lucian is the father you know.'

'Really, but the D.N.A test came back as negative didn't it? That pic that I saw of him a few weeks ago, I thought then he does look a bit like Lucian.'

'I know she has begged him to do another test, but he won't.'

'Why do you think it could be wrong?'

'Could be,' come on she looks like she's struggling a bit there.'

'Aw did you see the pic of Amelia?'

'Yeah Cassy did show me it, born early wasn't she. Hello, Miss Linane?' Kyle put out his hand as Miss Linane reached out hers and dropped some of her books. She looked familiar to Kyle.

'Mr. Bailey, Kyle Bailey and this is Miss Ryan, Alora. Come here let's give you a hand.'

'Thank you, my name's Jenna, Jenna Linane,' She smiled she knew all about Kyle Bailey, a.k.a Mr. Bailey formerly a teacher at Waverly Secondary. She was in the sixth form when he was a young new teacher. He was still gorgeous and them green eyes with his dark thick eye lashes they were so unusual; he wasn't a pretty boy he was more rugged but definitely had got better with age.'

'Nice to meet you Jenna, come on we will show you the ropes.' Kyle responded kindly as he tried to figure out how he knew that name.

'Morning Mr. Bailey.' One of the mums dropping off her son at pre school early, greeted Kyle with a childlike giggly good morning, while totally ignoring Alora and Jenna.

'He's still got it then,' Jenna thought.

'Thank you.'

After a couple of days Sadie and Amelia were both ready to go home. Lucian had taken parental leave, and Cassy was enjoying running Lucian's office while he was out of the office. Lucian had only rung once so far, he had left his diary on his desk, he asked Cassy to let him know if there were any important appointments that he should be aware of. Cassy enjoyed sitting in Lucian's office, she felt more important and hoped to be able to have her own office when she got the job that Lucian was advertising through the agency for an office manager, all internal employees had been invited to apply. Cassy had already filed her application last week. She filled him in with a couple of appointments, before he asked her to put his diary in the draw in his desk and lock his office. She discovered a CV laying in his desk drawer.

Mia Malone Business Manager

There was a yellow post it note attached to the plastic covering on her CV.

Mia start date October 2nd

Sadie was enjoying motherhood, she was a 'natural,' so the midwife had told her. Lucian was loving his new baby daughter also, and would do his fair share of nappy changing and singing Amelia or 'Milly' as he often called her to sleep. He had been impressed with how Sadie had taken to motherhood and how she was up in the night feeding Amelia while he slept. Sadie's focus had changed, and her priorities had changed, she was no longer distrusting of Lucian and wondering about his whereabouts, she had more important things to do. Sadie and Lucian grew closer, they were both more tired naturally, but appeared to both be happy and content. For the first few weeks until Lucian announced that he had employed Mia.

Sadie was fuming with Lucian. *'How could he? After all they had been through, Mia of all people, time for the tracker to make its appearance again!'*

Mia's CV stood out from the rest. He already knew her capabilities and her contacts, he knew there would be a few that wouldn't be happy with his choice of office manager, but tough, he thought, he was a businessman, and it was *his* business, and he was sticking to his decision, end of.

*

Christmas

'Did you ring your friend to see if the trees are ready to buy yet?'

'Not since the last time you asked Sade, he said they would be ready the second week of December and it's only the 1st today,' Lucian said over the sound of Amelia's giggles as he was blowing raspberries on her tummy.

'Look how fast she is now Luce, haha she is crawling at a speed, I'm telling you she will be walking soon, Rachel at the mum and baby group, her son is a week older than Amelia and he's not even crawling yet, clever girl aren't you and yes grandma and grandad are going to have you at theirs tonight aren't they.'

'Ok great, she is a clever one aren't you Milly.'

'Morning Mr. Bailey.'

'Morning.'

Alora giggled. 'She so fancies you.'

'Shut up, which one?'

'Ha both of them, it's so obvious I think that's why she comes in the playground all dressed up and full make up every morning.'

'Well, I can't help it can I, glad to know I have still got it haha, 'Hi Jenna.'

'There's another.' Alora mumbled to herself.

'Hi Kyle,' Jenna the new young teacher had started calling Kyle by his first name, she had been so used to calling him Mr. Bailey, from when she was in sixth form and luckily for him, he hadn't recognised her. She had joined the sixth form in the last few months that Kyle had been teaching, due to her parents moving down from up north. She still held her northern accent, so she hadn't bothered telling Kyle she had been one of the sixth from students at the school he once taught at, Waverly Secondary school. He was still gorgeous though, she thought to herself smiling back, all the girls used to fancy him and so did half of the mums, and so did a lot of the mums here. Some had even been to watch him play bass in his band when he played locally, however she had decided not to mention recognising him from her previous school.

'Anyway, how's you and Cassy now?'

Kyle stared at Alora; his smile dropped immediately. 'Sorry it's not my place, ignore me.' She apologised awkwardly.

'Ah no it's okay, anyway you and she are getting pally again I hear? She said she was going back to yoga classes with you in the week?'

'Yes, I have missed it.'

'What the yoga or you and Cassy?'

'You are so funny Kyle but to answer your question, even though you didn't answer mine, yes both actually, Cassy and the yoga.'

'Okay my bad, yes we are okay 'ish' at the moment thank you, you know getting on okay and well that's it. What about you and Blake?' The awkward silence returned for a second and Alora ignored his gaze.

'Same, you know, ticking along he has been off the

drink for months now and just thrown himself into work, he's been doing a lot of work for Lucian as they are both in the motor trade.' They had both reached the staff room and Alora was consciously aware of the staff room chitter chatter gossip, in which she called it and changed the subject quickly.

'Your turn to make the morning coffee Kyle.'

'But what about going to parties and that, how do you manage that with Blake the way he is?' Kyle asked with a louder voice than he realised he had as always.

'I manage, anyway make mine with an extra sugar this morning please?' Alora tried changing the subject again, she didn't want to talk about it, and certainly not here, but life had been a little all work and no play she admitted to herself, she'd had the odd trip to the pub with her work colleagues mainly Suzi and had called it a staff meeting to Blake. He had been doing so well lately however, it did mean that their social life just consisted of going to the cinema, mainly to watch films of Blake's choice or events where there wasn't any alcohol around, mainly time with Blake's kids or car shows. With Christmas looming she was a little worried of what could happen. Alora was still staying at her house for now and Blake at his, he hadn't mentioned the proposal for a little while, Alora wasn't ready for that yet, she wanted to see him sober for a couple of years first, as her father advised her. Michael, Alora's father didn't like Blake although he hadn't taken to any of Alora's previous boyfriends either. 'I'm not supposed to like your boyfriends Alora, I'm your father,' he always joked, but Alora was his only daughter, and he only wanted what was best for her. Michael hadn't liked Alora's first boyfriend Johnny, but that was only because Alora had been so young when they were dating, plus, he had seemed a bit of a Jack the lad and could sometimes distract Alora from her studies, he hadn't wanted Alora to fail her exams, but looking back he thought, he preferred him to this Blake one. At least with Johnny you knew where you stood, a bit of a cheeky chappie though.

'I wondered what happened to him Jenny?'

'Who Michael?'

'Johnny?'

'Johnny who?'

'Alora's Johnny?'

'Oh, *that* Johnny?'

Jenny smiled to herself as she dried the dishes and let her eyes wander onto the back garden. She thought back to the time when Alora and Johnny would sit chatting for hours with their strawberry milkshakes. She could picture them now and what a fine lad he was she smiled; she had liked Johnny.

'He moved back to Ireland with his mother Michael.' It amazed Jenny how Michael had been suffering with the onset of dementia but could remember things from years ago.

'I liked him,' Michael said, as Jenny rolled her eyes and started to prepare dinner. In her memory, Michael wasn't too keen on him at all or any one of Alora's boyfriends since.

'Well, Alora's with Blake now and they are coming to

dinner tonight, apparently Blake wants to ask you something.'

'Oh, does he now?' Michael's tone lowered.

'Blake fidgeted nervously on the doorstep and straightened the cellophane on the bunch of flowers he was carefully holding until he saw the outline of Alora's mother Jenny coming to the front door.

'Hello dear, do come in,' she beamed excitedly. She was hoping that Blake's visit was what she was thinking it was. 'Hello Jenny, these are for you.' Blake presented Jenny with a variety of colours, in a pretty rose medley bouquet.

'Aw thank you Blake, they are lovely,' she said as she inhaled the top of the bouquet as Blake followed her through to the lounge. 'Evening, …..no Alora?'

'Evening Michael, no I just wondered if I could have a few minutes of your time please?'

'Does Alora know you are here?' Michael asked as he reached for the tv remote and aimed it at the television to mute the sound.

'No, she…'

'Why on earth not?' Michael was slightly abrupt in his tone. 'Hang on love, Blake is here to talk to you, would you like a drink love, cup of tea or?' Jenny tried to calm the tension that was in the air created by her husband.

'Er no thank you, I will just come out with it,' Blake said nervously as he seated himself on the sofa to the left of Peter's armchair. I'd like to ask your permission of Alora's hand in marriage please?'

Present - London Borough Police Station

Wilson caught up with a very eager Jenkins in the corridor, 'so this just gets more interesting.'

'It certainly does,' Jenkins agreed, rubbing her hands.

'Apologies for my absence on the Cassy interview, seems like you got a little more out of her then?'

'That's okay and yes, as I said in the message, I got quite a lot of info to be honest,' Jenkins slightly bragged without intention, 'we got more than I thought we would out of that Cassy one, obviously not everything. I mean the two of them having an affair, it completely changes perspective, it could show the driver's incentive too and to why Alora is laying in intensive care.'

'Mmm 'If it's true.' Wilson replied, much to Jenkins's annoyance, 'well the truth will come out as you always say, Jenkins said sternly, 'round two, let's see what this one has to say then,' she took the lead to the interview room and Wilson followed.

Wilson looked steadily at the figure seated in front of him. 'For the benefit of the tape the date is June 26th, and the time is 19.32.'

'Okay, so you do know why you are here?'

'No comment.'

'For the benefit of the tape you have been arrested for the attempted assault on Alora Ede Ryan, who is currently still quite poorly and in the high dependency unit at the London Borough Hospital. Do you have anything to say?'

'What rubbish, that's why I have to say.'

Wilson shuffled his chair forward and glanced towards Jenkins.

'We have a witness in the name of Michael Ryan that has made a statement that suggests he caught you holding a pillow over his daughter, Alora Ryan's face, who is currently receiving medical care. What do you have to say to that Blake?' Jenkins asked, her glare not leaving Blake's face. 'Her father never liked me, he's lying, in fact he doesn't like anyone near his daughter, you do know he has dementia don't you, but anyway even before that, he was always an angry man, that's where Alora gets her temper from.' Wilson wondered if there was actually an element of truth in what Blake was saying, however he did not show this to either Blake or Jenkins instead he asked, 'Can you give me an example of Michael Ryan and Alora's temper please?'

'Yes.'

Present - London Borough Hospital

'Well, she has started to show signs of improvement, and she is gradually becoming more aware, this initially was just for a few seconds but last night it was over a couple of minutes. Her recent brain scan was clear, showing no abnormal swelling which is fantastic news. It is just going to be a case of ongoing physio for a while, obviously after having the operation on her back, but eventually in time, with youth on her side she should be back to where she was pre accident.'

'Thank you doctor that is great news.'

'No problem,' as he started to leave the room he turned around, 'Ah we have upped our security, due to last night's event and well, it appears that no damage has been done, but you know just to be on the safe side.'

'Great, thank you doctor appreciated, thanks again,' Jenny let out a huge sigh of relief, it was good news for her daughter and to her, that was the most important thing. She had not seen Blake holding a pillow over her daughter's face, as her husband Michael had entered the room first, however for her daughter's sake, she had to take her husband's allegations seriously.

Present time - Therapy

'And how long as she been abusing you Blake?'

'For about the same length of time, four or five years give or take a year, she has manipulated me as well for a while.'

'Could you give me an example?' Mr. Collins asked Blake as he excused his tickly cough.

'She knew I was giving up the alcohol mainly because I wanted to keep a clear head as alcohol doesn't suit her, she does things then doesn't remember them. Once I was trying to help her with her cooking and I think she was tired and she offered to cook some pasta, however I have an intolerance to it, so I helped her prepare a casserole which I think annoyed her and so she put red wine in our casserole, just to be spiteful and it made me feel so queasy, when I asked her about it she laughed.'

Mr Collins remained silent and waited for Blake to continue. 'Another time she threw a cup of coffee at me luckily it missed, but it hit her mirror in her lounge above her fireplace and it smashed, then she asked me to leave and rang her friends and pretended that I had done it; she is so good at acting and playing the victim.'

'Okay, interesting,' Mr. Collins replied before asking, 'why do you think she does these things Blake and how do you react?'

'I really don't know; all I have ever done is try and help her. I know her job can be stressful she is a schoolteacher you see, but nothing I ever do is right.'

'And how do you react?'

'Oh, sorry yeah, your last question, well I always try and calm her down, the coffee incident at the mirror, I just walked out and went home. I bought her a new mirror not long after as it was her birthday. She did apologise for her behaviour on that one and said she needed a break for a few days to get her head together, and things were good for a while and then it happened again.'

'Has she ever hurt you physically I mean?' Mr. Collins asked while cleaning his glasses. There was a pause for a while as Blake rubbed his chin and looked down to his right. 'Yes.'

'Okay can you describe to me exactly what she has done please?' 'She has hit me around the head before.' Mr. Collins eyebrows rose as he made some more notes.

'What lead up to her doing that, or did she hit you impulsively? I am not condoning, there are reasons why

I ask these questions Blake, I am building a picture of Alora, a pattern to her behaviour. Mr. Collins confirmed. 'Nothing major really, I think I was just watching the football one night while one of her favourite films was on, she had been drinking wine, and as I cheered because there was a goal, she threw a book at my head.'

'Johnny!' Alora screamed.

Chapter Seventeen

Present

'Aw you are back with us now Johnny, where did you go?' Alora asked as she was admiring Blaze, the chestnut horse in the field in front of her.

'Sorry Lor, there's a lot of work to be done here at Uncle Joe's farm, did you not see Jessie run off, she's the dark brown Irish Draught breed.'

'Irish Draught? They should have called her 'Guinness' or Ginny.' She laughed.

'She's a sod I was trying to coax her back into the field.'

'But she can't see you Johnny can she?'

'No, but horses are clever she could obviously feel me.' Johnny replied, he had also been to see his ma, but she wasn't at home, he had found her at the airport getting on a flight to England.

'I popped away quick to see me ma too Lor, just for a minute. Don't worry I was listening to your story; where was you, erm near Christmas and Blake was asking your dad for his permission for your hand in marriage?'

'Yeah that's right,' Alora replied a little glumly, 'so what would your ma be doing going to England Johnny?' Before Jonny could reply Alora found herself back at the

hospital, she could see her friend and work colleague
Suzi sitting at her bedside smiling, Alora smiled back and
managed a 'hiya.'

Johnny's mother crossed herself as she boarded her flight
from Dublin airport. It had been a while since she had
visited England. She had been back in Ireland for almost
ten years and had barely had any contact with her family
there since her cousin Jimmy passed away eight years
ago. She buckled herself into her seat and said a silent
prayer to herself.

Alora could hear her friend Suzi excitedly telling the
nurses how Alora had said 'hiya' to her. The nurses were
very pleased as 'That was the first time she had spoken.'
It was a surreal experience for Alora as the sound of the
nurse's voices started to fade simultaneously as Johnny's
voice started to resonate. She found herself with Johnny
at Uncle Joe's farm and climbed on Blaze. Johnny to her
left, his emerald eyes smiling in the glorious sunlight
matching the fields of green around them both.
    'Ah your back, come on Lor let's go follow me.'
    Johnny led the way as they rode through acres of
wooded pasture from the crunching of the branches to the
sound of the light wind whistling to the song of the bird.
As they rode out onto the open mountains. Alora felt a
wave of passion and freedom and rode like she was a
natural, even though she had never even sat on a horse
back home.
    Alora and Johnny both travelled through many places

in Ireland that day, through acres of green fields where the deeply satisfying scent of sunshine, sea air, meadow grass and leather had filled the air around them, to the coast of untouched golden sands and even into Dublin city, where they stood on the bridge of the River Liffey and then on to O'Neill's to gate crash a wedding where they danced and sang to a local band.

As the evening sun cast its shadow and the glimpse of the orange tinge in the sky started to show signs of the sun setting, it was the perfect moment Johnny thought, with the sky ablaze in front of them to kiss Alora. It was in that moment that Alora was determined to stay here with Johnny for as long as she possibly could.

Previously

'Well, I spoke to Sadie, she has bought Lucian a ticket and Kyle and Cassy are going, so I thought why not? me and you may go too, and we can all have a night out for old times' sake.' Blake suggested to Alora.

'Okay if you are up to it I mean, I said I would stay out of pubs and clubs along with you to help you stay off the drink and …'

Blake interrupted. 'I'll be fine.'

'Okay it's just that, well don't you think it's a little too soon after your works drink Christmas party I..'

'That was different Alora, I told you, I am the boss I had to go, and well I have apologised for that, I said I was sorry not that I can remember much but it was s blip.' Blake defended.

'Yes and you didn't help much Alora, he should have had something to eat before he went, they do an evening cookery class at the church on Tuesday evenings, Gwen's daughter goes, she loves it.' Sonia Blake's mum added.

Alora bit her tongue hard and shot Sonia a look, which was completely ignored.

'So, I will leave it up to you to look after my son please.' Sonia added annoying Alora even more as she pecked Blake on the cheek and waved goodbye to Alora in Blake's hallway on her way out.

'Bye darling, bye Alora.'

Blake's mum Sonia had blamed Alora for Blake's drinking at times, she had blamed Alora for a lot of things, and when Blake had drunk a little too much on his works night out, she said Alora should have gone to help him. On the night in question, after Blake had found himself in trouble and had contacted Alora she hadn't replied, 'It was obvious he was drunk and there would have been no reasoning with him' she had justified to Sonia.

Chapter Eighteen

Christmas The Stadium, Central London - The Tickers

As the angel illuminated high above Oxford Street, London's late-night shoppers were walking faster than the red buses and black cabs in traffic. It was the busiest Saturday of the year, the Saturday before Christmas and just two days before Christmas Eve. Musical theatre lovers and diners were revelling in the festive season, amongst an array of red and white Santa hats as Christmas carols filled the air and mulled wine was served.

The Tower hotel looking across London Bridge was fully booked, and six friends were hoping to enjoy a child and drama free twenty-four hours in London's West End at The Stadium. Starting at one of the most highly recommended top London restaurants belong to one of the UK's top television show Chefs.

The six of them had all arranged to meet in the hotel lobby at 7pm. The Tickers would be playing at around 9.30pm so there was plenty of time for a few drinks, some nice food and a long awaited catch up between the six of them.

The six of them.
Three couples.
One secret affair.
One secret kiss.
One blackmailer.
Two manipulators.
More than one victim. Friends? Debatable.

Yet, all of them looking glamourous, happy, and lucky to be seated and waited on at this top London restaurant on the busiest and most festive Saturday of the year, much to the envy, of the tired waitress that served them all, who insisted that this time next year she would be in a Monday to Friday, nine to five job.

The Pretenders

It was awkward, very awkward indeed and if there was an oscar for pretence this evening, it would be a tough choice, however the evening continued, and fake pleasantries were performed extremely well, so far so good.

The Secret Kiss

The chemistry between these two were as obvious as the colour red in a black and white film. Why the others hadn't noticed before was either because previously they had been so caught up in their own world or they had previously decided to at least try and hide their natural attraction.

The manipulators.

It was a tough competition between the two. Both scored ten out of ten for manipulation, however both delivered in separate ways. One was a little more devious than the other, if it was possible, and ever so slightly more honest about their manipulation process.

The Secret affair.

There was no secret, the blackmailer had put pay to that, albeit currently it was still just between the three of them. Chemistry? Yes, definitely, but hidden and not so obvious as the other's that had shared that kiss.

The blackmailer.

Most probably the one that was the most scared of their true colours being revealed. The over compliments to its victim were embarrassing to say the least and was noted.

The victims.

All of them, to a degree, one wasn't loved, one could only love themselves, the other couldn't love themself, one was loved too much, one loved for the wrong reason and more than one of them loved another person, other than their partner.

Sadie and Lucian were both enjoying a child free twenty-four hours and was already looking forward to the lay in bed in the morning in the hotel. Lucian had just closed for a week and had just sealed a huge deal which would mean expansion in the new year. Sadie was also happy to be able to wear her glamourous dress and not have to worry about baby sick or baby food over her clothes.

Cassy was in her element; she loved the band and she had almost ignored the others while she jumped around in her own little world. She wouldn't have cared who she was with tonight, this was her favourite band ever and she had missed out on their last tour a couple of years ago, due to her having a case of the flu.

Kyle, like Alora, had been busy at work and he was also looking forward to the holiday season and was enjoying a few beers and letting off some steam. He was happy to see Cassy enjoying herself and was looking forward to Christmas with Louie and his sister Lisa. He had also arranged to take Louie to see Father Christmas and promised Lisa at some point that they would take Louie to see their relatives in Ireland as he had received a friend request on social media from his Aunt Maggie who he had lost touch with previously.

Blake appeared to be glued to his phone for most of the evening as his gambling habit had taken a hold of him again after the promising tip off he had received earlier in the day. He did keep to his word of no alcohol all evening; however, he had been quite attentive to Alora when he wasn't on his phone and had patiently queued for over an hour at one point to buy her favourite cocktail that she liked.

Alora was contented, she could relax without worrying about Blake's drinking for once, as in her experience if he was going to drink it would usually have happened at the start of the evening, plus, school was closed, and she was looking forward to the holiday season.

The Tickers rocked the venue and towards the end of the set, they covered a couple of Christmas classics and the after-show party carried on until the early hours until they all decided to head back to the hotel.

The six of them.
Three couples.
One secret affair.
One secret kiss.
One blackmailer.
Two manipulators.

My Grandma always says you can count on one hand your true friends in life, I think maybe in some cases at a push two hands tops, and those people, those true friends are like gold. We will all meet many people in life that we class as friends but, in reality are perhaps just mere acquaintances. Those that you have surrounded yourself with and not always through choice. Your boss's wife, your brother's girlfriend, your colleague's partner, your colleague, your friend's sister, your lodger, your partner's boss and even perhaps your partner. The list is endless, yet on the flip side, your soul mate, the one you were meant to be with, could be right in front of your eyes. I will never settle for second best, and neither should you. Anonymous.

The affair

Her

'Merry Christmas.'

Him

'Merry Christmas.'

Her

'Nice hotel isn't it; I love hotels, I love having sex in hotel rooms on hotel beds, in fact I love sneaking into hotels and..'

Him

'You're drunk.'

Her

'So.'

Him

'Go to bed.'

Her

'I can't he's fast asleep and I can't sleep I'm bored.

Him

'Go and join him. I'm not doing this again.'

Her

'Doing what again? We have never been stuck in a lift together.'

Him

'We are not stuck, just take your finger off the button.'

Her

'Where are you going, what floor?'

Him

'I was going down to the bar ground floor.'

Her

'Is she down there?'

Him

'No, she's asleep, I couldn't get to sleep either, I needed a night cap.'

Her

She noted how he looked appealingly at her for a moment, however his eyes turned cold and distant.

'I can be you're night cap.' She suggested as she grabbed his hand and guided it up her skirt. She leant forwards onto him as the lift started moving, upwards. He tried to decline, but he was horny, and her hands told her so. In that split second before he touched her every nerve in her body electrified. The excitement of being caught was too much for him as he opened his trousers. His head was saying no, his body was saying yes as he pulled her on top of him and pushed her back up onto the mirrored wall of the lift. It was like a drug to them both and her back arched in anticipation, knowing that he would soon be inside her. He started to tease her telling her to 'beg' as he watched her body writhe. The lift now moving as he entered her and with every thrust she let out a moan.

As the lift came to a halt on the top floor, neither of them cared if anyone was watching in the heat of the moment, both their minds unable to process the pleasure fast enough.

No one was. They had been lucky this time.

Chapter Nineteen

Two and a half years later
One month before the accident

'Oh my god! a puppy! Thank you Kyle, I love him, it is a he isn't it?' Cassy squealed like a child.

'Yes he is a he Cassy, ten-week-old bless him.'

'Aw thank you I need to think of a name for him, he's gorgeous, what is he?'

'He's a dog Cass.'

'I know haha, I mean what breed?' Kyle moves out of the way while Cassy pretends to smack him with the puppy's paw, 'you are so cute you gorgeous little thing aw look at his face.'

'He's a chocolate roan working cocker spaniel, he will need a lot of looking after, a lot of walks he'll be a handful at first, they are working dogs, hence the name and he will be full of energy.'

Alora, was so envious, but she was aware that Blake had an allergy to dogs.

'He is absolutely gorgeous, he really is.' Alora admired excitedly.

'You need to think of a name now Cass, and buy a waterproof, you'll need it, he will need to go out daily in all kinds of weather. The nights are light now but come winter, it will be a different story, you know that don't you and on the odd occasion, when I have parents evening and when it's dark and cold you'll have to take him. I'm happy to do my share too of course.'

'I am going to have to go, I have started sneezing already, you ready Alora?' Blake asked.

'Yes, I'm coming, aw he's so cute isn't he.'

'Yep, but he's making me sneeze.'

'Aw Cass tell me when you've decided on a name please and send me some pics and vids later.' Alora asked as she stroked the puppy.

'Ah I think he's weeing!'

'Haha, we'll leave you to sort that, come on Blake.'

Cassy looked content Kyle observed as she sat there happily playing with the cute little chocolate brown pup. He had been pondering on the idea of getting a dog for a while now, Louie was four years old now and loved dogs. His mum Lisa wasn't really fussed, so this new pup was partly for Cassy, partly for Kyle and partly for Louie. Recently Cassy had declared that she never wanted children of her own, Kyle had shrugged it off initially, but he *did* want children, and the more time Kyle spent with Louie, the more his need to become a father grew stronger. The only family around him was his sister Lisa and his nephew Louie. He had a few cousins and aunties and uncles in Ireland too, but it was becoming an uncle that had confirmed it for him. He found it hard to understand anyone who did not want children, including

Cassy. He was aware that she hadn't had the greatest childhood. Cassy's mother Deana had fallen pregnant with Cassy at just fifteen years old while she was staying in the UK temporarily having travelled from her home in Australia. She was staying with her grandparents on her father's side for just one year. Deana's parents had been mortified and had flown to England to support Deana with the birth, then arranged for Cassy to be adopted, her young mother had no say in the matter. Cassy was in contact with her natural father for a while, when she had tracked him down not long after her 16th birthday, however he had a snooty wife, twin boys and a daughter all under six and Cassy hadn't felt particularly welcome. Her father had told her that if she needed any money he would happily provide. Cassy didn't want his money; she had just wanted a family that loved her. Luckily, her adoptive parents had always supported her the best they could, however Cassy had gone off the rails slightly and they had adopted and fostered lots of children over the years and Cassy felt that she always had to fight for their attention and by the time she was seventeen she had rebelled and left home. Cassy's grandmother on her father's side had died when Cassy was only ten and her grandfather who she was still in touch with, lived thirty miles away north of London, in a quaint little village, he had wanted to escape the 'hustle and bustle' he had once said. She visited him every couple of years, and they sent each other birthday cards. She was close to one of her foster brothers Theo, being just one year younger than Cassy, they had both formed a bond with one another.

Cassy's mother married an Australian and wrote letters to Cassy, she never visited England and did at one point invite Cassy to Australia in a response to one of Cassy's letters, however Cassy had declined and decided to save the invite for when she really wanted to escape. She had now added her mother Deana on social media, and they would chat now and again, however to Cassy, Deana felt like a long-lost Aunt that she would catch up with from time to time. She watched the progress of her younger siblings on social media from both of her parents. Cassy envied those that had a 'normal' family she once said to Kyle, even though he had lost his mother tragically at a young age, and if anything for Kyle the experience had left him wanting a large family. He loved Louie and had spent every other weekend with him. He had been Louie's only male role model until recently and Louie did look similar in appearance to his uncle and people would often assume that Kyle was his father sometimes, the only difference being the eye colour, Louie's eyes were blue as opposed to Kyle's green.

Lisa had recently met what Kyle described as a 'decent guy' and he had hoped, for the sake of Lisa and Louie that he would stick around. Devon was his name and he had recently started working for Blake at his garage and Cassy had got chatting to him and arranged a blind date with him for Lisa. They had hit it off immediately and Lisa had told Cassy that she hadn't laughed that much in ages and now they were dating. Lisa had slowly introduced Devon to Louie at a day out to their local bowling alley. Devon's ancestors were from Jamaica, and he had promised to take Lisa and Louie there next year. He had a big family here in England and they started to treat Louie as one of their own.

Cassy still hadn't bonded with Louie, even though he was now four and starting school in September, it was almost as if she just tolerated him for the sake of Kyle sometimes, she had even felt 'left out' as she had told Kyle one weekend. She also suggested that he was being 'too spoilt' which Kyle didn't take too kindly to and told Cassy that if anything *she* was acting like a spoilt child and told her to 'grow up and stop being pathetic.' He had hoped the puppy would be a shared interest for both Cassy and Louie.

'Rolo, that's what I am going to call him.' Cassy decided.

'Right, Rolo it is then, come here little fella.'

'There's a clever girl! Aw did you hear that Lucian?' Sadie asked proudly, Amelia had read a few words from her new book that she had received as one of her birthday presents for her third birthday.

'Clever girl Milly, daddy is proud of you, well done.'

'Daddy will keep calling you Milly eh, silly daddy eh it's Amelia isn't it.'

'I like Milly.' Amelia piped up; I want to be called Milly not Amelia.'

'So do I darling.' Lucian agreed admiring his beautiful daughter. 'Wow you did get a lot of presents didn't you, you lucky girl.'

'Yes she did, and you deserve it don't you darling. I will arrange all of her presents soon, there are too many in the dining room, I will put her favourite ones in her bedroom and the others in her playroom. Talking of which I was thinking of arranging a dinner party soon, mum and dad said they would have Amelia at theirs.' Lucian's face dropped.

'Come on Lucian, it will be fine third time lucky and all that, since I was a little girl I dreamt of having my own house and throwing a dinner party.

'Yes and look what happened with the last two.'

'Isn't daddy a grump eh?' Sadie moaned to Amelia in her baby voice. 'Well, I have messaged the others and they are all free for a month this Saturday the 2^{1st}, I thought it would be nice, it's been a while and now you have promoted Cassy, plus you and Blake are both putting business each other's way. I also wouldn't mind speaking to Alora about Boadfield Primary for Amelia and..'

'Oh, I get it; I knew there would be something in it for you Sade.'

'For our daughter Lucian.' Sadie corrected him with a glare. 'It's a good school and hard to get into and I have applied but I just have some questions, she will be starting next year won't you darling?'

'Yes mummy, I start school.'

'Yes darling clever girl, I will give you a hand with the menu so is that a yes then daddy?' Sadie asked in her baby voice.'

'Okay but maybe a barbeque, and no drama's please.'

'Aw I really want a puppy now Blake.' Alora blurted out on the car ride home from Cassy and Kyle's.

'I'm allergic Alora you know that.' Blake replied as he sat at the lights, urging them to go green so he could get home and take an antihistamine.'

'I know that, but not hypoallergenic ones and we don't currently live together, I have been googling we could get a poodle, a cockerpoo or even a labradoodle would be okay?'

'Too much going on at the minute, we work too many long hours, it's okay for Cassy she works from home sometimes and you don't.'

'True, talking of Cassy, she said Sadie and Lucian are having a gathering apparently a month on Saturday 21st.

'Are they, okay cool.' Blakes tone changed to a more positive one.

'Hopefully, there will be no drama.' There was silence for a few moments.

'Bless you,' Alora said to Blake as he sneezed.

'Aw jeez, Lor they never did they? They held dinner party number three; did they not learn from the first two and what were you still doing with that Eejit anyway?'

Alora had left Blake a couple of times in the last two years, but he somehow managed to persuade her to go back to him. He had remained sober for a while, and they had started to gradually socialise and Alora had to no longer avoid social situations. They remained to live in separate households, which was Alora's choice.

Present

The Driver

His time was up. He had to face it. The last person he had wanted to hurt, he *had* hurt and now it was about to be exposed.

He took a deep breath and opened his eyes.

'I have to caution you; you are under arrest for leaving the scene of the accident and causing considerable damage to both the victim's car and the victim. 'Are you aware of this?'

'Yes, and I am, and I am so very sorry.'

The affair

Her

She was no longer that girl, who dared to dream of her and her lover ending up in a 'happy ever after' situation. She had become wiser, and she knew that he was never going to leave her friend. She had suggested it once and the look on his face had told her more than his words ever could.

Him

He could no longer blame the lack of love and support from her at home for his actions. What had started as a bit of fun, was now becoming the norm.

Him and Her

Initially the affair began as a distraction, which had happened when both her and him were stressed at home, an escapism for them both. Neither wanted to cheat on their partners, they just wanted some relief from the existing burden of responsibilities, both offering each other a distraction from the grey reality of domestic stress. Currently, the affair had just become part of their double life. For him and her, their emotional and physical needs were now met with one and other. While their familiar needs along with their need for security were met with their original partners. They both had now become experts in manipulation and also experts at lying and deceiving, which says more about the weakness of the two. Both, have exceedingly high sex drive's and find it hard to say no to temptation. Unfortunately, for them both, their secret is about to be uncovered and statistically only 5 – 7% of affairs end in the couple involved forming a relationship after exposure. Luckily, the majority of people are trustworthy and faithful and will never be tempted or be the victim of such deceit and for her, she had now had enough and intended to end it, and if he could be bothered, then so would he.

Chapter Twenty

Previously

'Ding Dong'

'Hiya Kyle, hiya Cassy, mwah mwah do come in, thank you.' Sadie greeted with two air kisses and a slightly awkward presence. She hadn't seen Cassy for a while, and she would never openly show or air her true feelings about Kyle.

'How are you both? You are looking well, both of you.'

'Okay thanks yes, you?' Cassy responded with equal awkwardness, while Kyle nodded and grinned as he followed the burning smell of barbeque and made his way towards a welcoming Lucian, waving his grill fork as a greeting.

'Ooh my favourite red, thank you, would you like a glass?' Sadie asked Cassy as the two women avoided gaze until the wine was poured and they both 'cheered' their drink.

'Oh Kyle, there's some house shoes there, for when you have been in the garden and want to come back into the house,' Sadie advised Kyle when he tried to enter the conservatory from the garden to grab him and Lucian a beer, 'you can wear your own shoes for the garden, but please pop the slip-on shoe on to enter back in the house, the men's sizes are in the box on the left.' Both Cassy and Kyle burst into a fit of giggles simultaneously.

'Ding Dong.'

'Heya both come in mwah Alora you look lovely, love your dress and you look well, both of you.' Sadie lied, she thought Blake looked drained with his prominent dark circles under his eyes.

'Thank you, mmm something smells nice.' Blake said as he wandered off to the garden with his bottle of J20 to join the men.

'So how are you Alora? I do love that dress where is it from?'

'I got it in the sale last summer thank you, can't remember where. How's you?'

'Good thanks, loving life with Amelia and being a parent still and...' Sadie thought she would start early with her charm and the info that she needed from Alora to try and secure a child's place for Amelia starting school next September.

'Ding Dong.'

'Hello Mia, do come in.' There was no air kiss between the two ladies, just a very quick eye up and down of Mia's sophisticated business-like suit, with a pretty white blouse underneath.

'It's informal dress wear darling, did I not mention it to you?' Mia looked at her with a blank expression and then handed Sadie her expensive suit jacket to hang up like she was handing it to a cloak attendant and wiggled her way straight to the garden while placing the bottle of white on the island in the kitchen as she passed.

Lucian almost dropped his barbeque fork that was holding his burger onto the garden patio when he caught sight of Mia heading towards him, very closely followed by Sadie.

'Hi guys.' Mia said confidently to all as she felt everyone's eyes on her. She had previously met the majority of them, briefly.

Lucian remained lost for words for a couple of seconds until Sadie broke the silence as if reading his mind.

'I invited Mia Lucian, I thought we may be able to put some business each other's way.'

Alora rolled her eyes quickly at Cassy managed a wry smile back at her while secretly enjoying the awkwardness. Lucian looked like he wanted to kill Sadie there and then. 'Okay hi Mia.' He managed.

'I'm going to kill her.' Lucian thought angrily, a little blushed and flustered and barely managing to fake a smile.

'What is she playing at? Why didn't she just bloody tell me that she had invited Mia, does she want me to look like a total twit or what?' Lucian wanted to march Sadie back into the house, but he refrained as all eyes appeared to be on him.

'Will Christie be joining us Mia?' Everyone in the garden waited for her response and assumed Christie was her partner.

'Yes Lucian, he is still working at the moment, but hopefully he will be joining us,' she looked at her watch and Sadie noted how slender her arms were, 'probably around 4pm ish, a couple of hours he said, but thanks anyway, for inviting us.'

Mia wasn't stupid, she knew when she received the text message last night that Lucian had no idea that Sadie had invited her and her partner Christie, however she had no other specific plans this weekend and it was a beautiful sunny Saturday.

'Okay great.' Lucian croaked and faltered mid-note, he cleared his throat and made his excuses to pop back to the house to grab a glass of water.

'Anyone else coming today?' Alora asked Sadie, the sarcasm was completely wasted on Sadie, Alora noted.

'No Alora, everyone's here now.' There was no way Sadie was going to have any confrontation today, not in front of the lovely Mia. 'Oh, sorry there maybe just one more, Mia's partner when he arrives, Christie is it?' Sadie asked keenly as she turned to Mia.

'Yes.' Mia confirms with a nod of her head.

'So, Mia sorry, would you like a drink? Follow me.' She bossed. 'So how long have you been with Christie?'

'Thanks, a wine would be nice, I prefer red, and we have been dating for a few weeks now, Christie and I, to answer your question.'

'A girl after my own heart, I prefer a red too.' Sadie replied while nodding her head to Mia as if approving her reply as the two ladies headed to the kitchen, just as Lucian was on his way back out to the garden to attend the barbeque.

'I don't know what Sadie is playing at inviting Mia without notifying me, but there will be something I'm sure, did you know she was invited Cass?'

'No, I had absolutely no idea, but apparently she was only invited last night so.., anyway Kyle has taken over your cooking, so I'd check them burgers before they are burnt haha,' Cassy casually changed the subject, while she pulled her sunglasses back down to her eyes, she was trying to hide her obvious pleasure watching Sadie trying to befriend Mia. It was obvious to Cassy what Sadie was doing.

There had always been a question mark back at the office hanging over Lucian and Mia's little business trip away, did they or didn't they? Unbeknown to them, it was the talk of the office while they were away.

Within two hours, the sun was shining, the sky was blue, and the music was playing amongst the chatter and laughter of all the guests. Christie had still not arrived, and Mia made her way to the bottom of the garden to call him.

Sadie received a couple of pictures from her parents of Amelia playing happily on the park swings and another one of her enjoying an ice cream. Sadie smiled and proudly showed the recent pictures to all, before pouring herself another glass of red. She decided to approach Alora again and talk children.

'Aw she is gorgeous Sadie, such a cute smile.'

'Thank you, I know I am bias but, ya know.' Sadie replied beaming with pride as she sat down in the shaded area of the patio next to Alora.

Sadie started to scroll through her camera roll of pictures of Amelia's birthday party and odd pictures taken since her birth as Alora looked on happily until one

one picture caught Alora's attention. 'Hang on that picture there, is that?' Sadie quickly scrolled her camera roll backwards and glanced at Alora uncomfortably while faking a giggle. Guilt was written all over Sadie's face as she tried to feign coolness. It didn't work.

Chapter Twenty-one

'That picture there?' Alora pointed to Sadie's phone.

'What picture? It's an old one, it's nothing.' Sadie replied as a worried expression pulled across her face. She closed her phone and stood up and headed towards the conservatory and Alora followed her.

'Shoes.' Sadie pointed down to the box as they approached it.

'Never mind the shoes,' Alora said impatiently, 'show me your phone I saw a picture let me have a look.'

Sadie headed towards the downstairs toilet, gripping her phone tightly, trying her best to get away from Alora, they both passed Lucian and Kyle who were opening beers from the fridge in the kitchen.

Alora's voice now raised louder. 'Sadie!'

'Hey what's going on you two, what's up?' Sadie froze on the spot, her face reddened..

'She's got a picture on her phone Lucian, and I've just seen it and now she is trying to delete it.'

'Sadie? Lucian knew she had something to hide, what's Alora talking about what is it?'

Kyle looked at Alora and back at both Sadie and Lucian with a slightly worried expression.

'Lucian it's nothing, I don't know what Alora saw I need to go to the toilet please!' As Sadie turned her back she felt a hand on her tightly gripped phone.

'What are you doing give me that back!'

'Sadie if you have nothing to hide you will let me have a look through your phone.' Lucian said angrily, he knew he had been previously tracked, and he had never looked at Sadie's phone, but he knew with Sadie there was no smoke without fire. By this time with the raised voices, Cassy, Blake, and Mia had all joined them. Sadie marched back through the hallway past the kitchen and conservatory and back out to the garden, with all eyes on her followed closely by Lucian. He approached her on his own.

'Could you just give us a minute guys please?' He turned to the others. 'Sadie can you for once be honest and tell me what it is you are trying to hide?' He asked calmy and passed her phone back.

'Sadie sighed, she knew she had been caught red handed and scrolled back down to the picture in question.

'Alright well here we go, you are not going to like this all of you,' she shouted in a harsh tone, but here goes!' Her hands were trembling by now as she took a sip from her large glass of red and held out the picture on her phone to Lucian, closely followed by Alora.

Lucian's eyes widened followed by the others behind him who were all curious to see what the picture was, they didn't have to wait long. 'What is that? It looks like a picture of two people kissing in a car, hang on…. its Alora and Kyle? Okay Sadie please explain.'

'Sadie?'

Sadie felt sick. She needed to think quickly if she was going to get out of this one. There was a stunned silence from all of them. Lucian, Alora, Cassy, Blake, Kyle, and Mia all standing there waiting in anticipation.

'I don't know, it was sent to me.'

'Who sent it?'

'I don't know it was from an anonymous number.' Sadie declared.

'Can I see the picture please?' Alora asked, bravely, Sadie thought. The picture was in fact of Alora in the driver's side of her car leaning over to Kyle very closely.

'Have you seen this Kyle?' She said almost snatching the phone from Sadie, 'Me and you in the picture, leaning over to you giving you a peck on the cheek and we were being watched, filmed and photo shopped by the look of it!' Kyle rubbed his hands through his long dark curls.

'I don't even remember this, when was it taken?'

'It was ages ago and..' Sadie started to justify.

'Let us have a look!' Blake interrupted as he took Sadie's phone from Alora and enlarged the picture with his fingers. 'Hmm looks more than a peck to me Alora!' Blake was white as a sheet, his hands had started trembling, and he felt an intense pang of jealousy and in that moment he wanted to swing for Kyle.

'It has been photo shopped Blake! It was just a peck on the cheek and..' Alora snapped.

'I didn't realise, that when you two car shared on the odd occasion to work, that you gave each other kisses Alora, peck on the cheek or not!'

Blake couldn't contain himself any longer and grabbed Kyle and tried to push him backwards onto the fence, however Kyle grabbed both of his arms with all his force and stopped him in his tracks.

'Right, you listen here, yes sometimes I give Alora a peck on the cheek and vice versa cos sometimes Blake, you have put her through hell even though she tries her best to hide it and get through the day at work, so yes sometimes I kiss your woman!' Kyle finally let go of Blake and Cassy noted the look of appreciation on Alora's face to Kyle and something inside of Cassy flipped.

'But that's not all is it guys!' Even Cassy was shocked at her own loudness and quietened down slightly. 'There has been a lot more going on hasn't there Sadie?' If looks could have killed Cassy would have been dead on the spot. Sadie tried her best to hush Cassy with her eyes and the stern look on her face, even though all eyes were now on Sadie, again. It didn't work.

'Come on Sadie show us the other pictures you have on your phone, in fact come on this is a moment for all of us to finally be fucking honest, I mean what a fast, what a fake friendly bubble we all live in, who wants to go first?'

*

Chapter nine continued ...

Cassy's interview

Previously

Present - London Borough Police Station

Cassy, I just want to ask you a few questions regarding your friendship with Alora.' Wilson said in his calming voice. Cassy thought he had one of them voices that should be narrating a wildlife programme, not quite David Attenborough, maybe a younger version, but still calming.

'In your statement it says you met at Boadfield Primary, five years ago is that correct?'

'Yes about then, five years.'

'And you became such good friends, you moved in with Alora at her house.'

'As a lodger yes, for a while.' Cassy responded emphasising 'lodger.'

'Okay, and then you moved in with Kyle Bailey?'

'Yes, well my stuff was still at Alora's for a while, but I used to stay at Kyle's a few nights a week when we got you know more serious.' Cassy responded sipping her water from the plastic cup in front of her, she kept her gaze at Wilson while feeling the glare from Jenkins.

'Okay and then you moved out of Kyle's for a while, so can I ask, with your belongings still at Alora's why you didn't move back in there instead of….' Wilson pauses to look at his notes, 'Bington Road?'

Cassy breathed a heavy sigh.

'Okay, you want to know why?' Wilson waited and Jenkins shuffled her chair in an inch forward.

'Because Alora was getting a little too close to Kyle.'

'Could you elaborate please?'

'She was seen kissing him in her car and god knows what else. I think they may have had a one-night stand, well, so I was told, but it wouldn't surprise me, so that's why I didn't go back.' Cassy raised her eyebrows at Wilson and awaited a response, while Jenkins either cleared her throat genuinely or she was talking in some kind of code to Wilson, Cassy decided.

'Okay so I am guessing you didn't see this with your own eyes, so who told you that this took place between them both?' Wilson sat back and rubbed his chin.

'It was Sadie, Sadie Johnson.'

Chapter Fourteen continued ...

Present - London Borough Police Station

Wilson and Jenkins both looked at Blake as if it to say, 'please elaborate.' There was no need. Blake barely stopped for a breath.

'I told you Alora is troubled, she takes after her father, he is a very angry man, and he doesn't like anybody near his daughter, not me not anyone ever! He even drove her first boyfriend back to Ireland and Alora is just as angry and crazy as he is. No! I wasn't putting a pillow over her face I was merely trying to make her comfortable, Alora sleeps with a certain pillow at home, because she is that fussy she won't sleep at mine unless she brings it and I wanted her to be comfortable, her dad saw me visiting her and he didn't like it, he has dementia you know, do you know that? So, if you want to listen to an angry man who's not in the right frame of mind, who also doesn't like anyone near his Princess Alora including me, then go ahead!' Blakes solicitor tried to interrupt with a cough, it didn't work. 'And, for the record no matter what I do for Alora, she wouldn't appreciate it because her father has spoilt her rotten in an overprotective even *weird* kind of way. I even had to ask him for permission to propose to her because she turned me away the first time, because the setting wasn't romantic enough. Ha did you know that?' It was a rhetorical question. 'You know what? You can ask Alora when she comes round, although she will deny it. I have put up with her lies and her cheating, her 'playing the victim,' Both Wilson and Jenkins followed Blake's fingers displaying air quotes, 'her treating me like a punch bag and basically being neurotic for years.' Blake let out a sigh and was welcomed with pure silence.

Chapter Twenty-two

'Come on Sadie, lets show the other pictures you have on your phone, in fact, come on this is a moment for all of us to finally be fucking honest, I mean what a fast, what a fake friendly bubble we all live in, who wants to go first?'

'Right, we all need to calm down a bit please.' Lucian suggested, however Cassy continued. 'Come on Sadie let's have you, show us what you have got, or I will. It's about time the truth came out, so I am going to go first. Lucian sit down and have a beer and..'

'Cassy what the hell are you doing?' Kyle asked, 'come on we are all here trying to have a good time, there has been a little too much alcohol consumed and ..'

'Lucian congratulations!' Cassy interrupted totally ignoring Kyle.

Lucian stood there frozen, with his hands open in a shrugged like expression waiting for Cassy, as were the others, to elaborate.

'Congratulations for what Cassy?'

'Louie is your son; you have a son, his name is Louie, ask your lovely girlfriend Sadie!'

Previously...

Sadie excitedly opened the envelope that had been hand delivered to her at work. Mrs. Thomas could wait a second, she had already been moaning that Sadie was running five minutes late, but this was so much more important.

'Just excuse me for one second Mrs. Thomas, would you like a coffee?' Sadie asked as she raced towards the back of the salon without awaiting Mrs. Thomas's reply carrying the envelope.

'No thank you I have already had two, I just need my nails done before half past thank you!' Mrs. Thomas could be heard shouting over the noise of the hairdryer behind her.

Sadie opened the letter and read the words that were like music to her ears. She read them again and again, until Katie one of her juniors came up to Sadie and politely told her that Mrs. Thomas had left the salon. Sadie didn't care, which was extremely unlike her. She re read for the last time as soon as Katie had gone back through to the salon.

'Lucian Taylor is excluded as the biological father.'

'Perfect.' Sadie was absolutely delighted with the copy. It was almost identical to the actual result that had arrived a few days ago. It was identical apart from the result on the genuine copy, previously received which stated.

'Lucian Taylor is not excluded as the biological father.'

Sadie had originally felt sick when she had opened Lucian's original results. She had cried and cried. She had just met the love of her life, the one man that she actually really wanted, the one man that had kept her on her toes, the one man that wouldn't give in to her demands, and the one man that she wanted to marry, have children with and grow old together with, and within an instant of opening that letter, Lucian's D.N.A results, she knew that she wouldn't be playing happy families for long. Her hormones were everywhere, and she needed to do something drastic, and drastic it was. She had crossed that line and there was no turning back. Sadie had almost changed her mind at the last minute, she knew that if Lucian ever found out what she had done it would be over, however she was in too far now, in too deep, so she proceeded to burn the remains of the original D.N.A results in the garden of her salon. She used one of her employees lighters that was left in the staff room. The remains of the letter went into the fire burner, and she washed her hands, told her staff she was popping out to the bank, but headed to post the results in the post box instead. When it arrived the next day, Sadie casually put the letter with another and waited patiently for Lucian to arrive home. She harboured her feelings of a mixture of guilt and relief. It became a daily habit for Lucian to check his post.

'Hi love. how's your day been?' Sadie asked Lucian in her high bubbly jubilant voice. '*She seems in a better mood than she was yesterday, considering I am meant to be going away on this business trip without her tomorrow.'* Lucian was still wondering how the hell Sadie knew that Mia had booked the flights for them. Sadie had no contact with Mia and Cassy didn't know that Mia had booked the flights, he even asked her today to double check. The only conclusion Lucian had come to was that perhaps Sadie had read his work emails somehow. Lucian hadn't changed his mind about Sadie joining them on the trip to Germany, especially after Sadie posting photos on social media of what should have been personal professional business meetings, plus, he hadn't liked her behaviour when she has had a little too much to drink and her being sick over potential clients.

'Yes not bad thanks, I have been busy, and I have been preparing for this meeting in Germany for tomorrow.' Lucian replied cautiously however he thought he would let Sadie know that he wasn't going to change his mind, she would just have to trust him with Mia. It was business and that was it.

Sadie's face dropped for a moment, however as soon as she told Lucian she was pregnant and as soon as he received the results of his D.N.A, she thought, she was certain that he would change his mind about leaving her and going away on this trip. She realised her timing was a bit lousy, but then again in a way she thought it was perfect, she smirked.

'Yes I bet you have been busy,' Lucian wasn't sure whether there was a hint of sarcasm there but didn't really care as his eyes wandered to the two letters on the kitchen work top and without thinking he opened the one from the top.

'You ok love?' Sadie asked. Lucian's face had dropped slightly. He had not been aware that he would feel the disappointment that he had, but there it was in black and white, he was not the biological father to Louie. He shared the news with Sadie, he knew she would be pleased. 'Well, you were right, according to this I am not Louie's father.'

'Oh no bless you, come here give us a hug, you ok?' Sadie played the innocent very well and comforted Lucian with a hug.

'Yep, I'm fine,' Lucian lied, he wasn't fine at all, but he would be, 'it is what it is,' Sadie overheard Lucian telling his friend Jez later on the phone. He now had to find out how the hell Sadie knew that Mia was booking the flights and concentrate on telling Sadie that it would be just himself and Mia going on the business trip to Germany as he reflected on him and Sadie's previous conversation.

'It's a business trip Sadie.'

'I know that don't worry; I can go shopping while you do all your boring stuff.' Sadie suggested. *'Come on Lucian spill, tell me about Mia!'* It was as if he read her thoughts.

'Thing is, it will be the three of us, me, you and Mia. You met her Saturday night, she works for..'

'Hmm blonde, tall, botoxed lips that one? Yeah I remember. That's fine Lucian. Tell her to book my flight too.' *'Hang on how did she know Mia was booking our flights?' Lucian wondered.*

Lucian rarely used the laptop at home, it was mainly used for Sadie's purchasing, he decided to have a look to see if there were any way that his work emails had been sent to his personal ones. He typed in the password. It was the wrong password, he tried again, still no joy.

'Sadie have you changed the password on the laptop?'

'Fuck, why does he want that?' Sadie had to think on the spot.

'Yeah I was getting lots of spam and there seemed to be a virus on there, why what are you after love?' Sadie lied far too easily.

'Okay, I just need the new password then.' Lucian replied suspiciously.

'It's embarrassing.' Sadie faked a laugh.

'What do you mean it's embarrassing Sadie what is it? I need to get into it?'

'I will type it in for you Lucian.' Sadie was panicking now.

'Sadie just tell me it please.' Lucian's tone was more serious.

'It's 'Ilovelucian84''

'It doesn't work Sadie.'

'Here let me please?' Sadie typed it again and it didn't work.

'Let me try it.' Lucian sat back down, he knew Sadie too well, she would have had to use a capital L from Lucian, they had had this conversation before, so he started to type.

'IloveLucian84' Still no joy. He tried again.

'ILoveLucian84' He was in. 'Thank you Sadie.'

Sadie was about to have a shower, however she decided to hover around in the kitchen, just in case she hadn't been as careful and had missed an email or not deleted something in her purchasing history. She was usually careful in removing anything she didn't want Lucian to see, but with her head focusing on the pregnancy and the D.N.A results, she may have been careless, although a lot of her secret purchasing was done at the salon.

Her purchasing history had been cleared; Lucian noted apart from a couple of items that appeared to be for the salon. He didn't have Sadie's email password and he would never go through anyone's personal emails, however on this occasion his morals left him. He tried to sign into her email account using the same password. No joy. She was too clever for that, so he went back onto his personal emails. There were a few different promotions from sites that he had barely used. Nothing interesting, he scrolled back further to the last few weeks and there was a thank you, for sharing his location history and an update to all his whereabouts from his 'timeline.' Lucian never shared his location on his phone, ever.

'She had been tracking him, he just knew it! But how the hell did she know that Mia had booked the flights?

Lucian always booked flights himself, whether it was for business or pleasure, even though he did have enough staff to do this for him and Sadie was well aware of this as it was an unwritten rule for Lucian since a mistake was made by Katrina his receptionist where she had booked the wrong airport two years ago. It had caused so much bother for him and his business, and ever since then, he decided that he would take control of any flight bookings. That was until Mia offered, she was very efficient he trusted her and, there had been a slight element of guilt for not booking Sadie on the trip, that subconsciously he thought if Mia booked the flights and the hotel it would ease his conscience, slightly.

Lucian wasn't sure why his instinct had decided to take him up the stairs to the bedroom where Sadie's phone was charging while she was in the bathroom.

Sadie didn't know whether it was stress or nerves or the pregnancy, but she had a sudden urge to be sick, she had heard of evening sickness before and was soon ready to tell Lucian she was pregnant anyway, but whenever she was sick, she would run the cold tap to drown out any noise, it was a habit she had and used anytime she used the bathroom.

Lucian could hear the cold tap running as he picked up Sadie's phone and sat down on his bed. He decided to ring the office reception number knowing that no one would answer as he was the last to leave the office. At the same time Sadie's number rang from an unknown number, he could hear the office message from his phone's handset and when he picked up Sadie's handset he could hear exactly the same.

Sadie knew she had been caught when she came back into the bedroom and found Lucian holding both his and her phone.

Lucian had confronted her instantly and she tried to lie at first, until he threatened to call the police. She cried and begged him not to before blaming her hormones by blurting out that she was pregnant and showing Lucian the pregnancy tests, all three of them. Lucian hadn't believed a word she had said, and at one point he had suggested that if she was pregnant it probably wasn't his anyway, after her little disappearing act at The Palace opening.

In his haste and anger, he made Sadie admit everything about her tracking devices and undo all the tracking at the same time. He secured his phone, blocked her number, and packed his bag for his business trip and checked into a hotel for the night. He was so angry, it wasn't until later at the hotel bar when he had slightly calmed down, the realisation that Sadie may actually be carrying his baby hit him hard.

What a day, he thought, he had found out he wasn't the father to his ex-girlfriend Lisa's baby and then found out that his girlfriend Sadie maybe pregnant, yet she was also a 'neurotic, jealous, stalking, over possessive, lying bitch,' he had told the young man the other side of the hotel bar, when it was just the two of them at last orders.

'And I thought I had had a difficult day,' was his reply.

Lucian laid back on the bed that evening in his hotel room staring at the television in a daze. He felt very hurt inside, hurt at the fact that Sadie hadn't trusted him, he loved her, and they generally got on well, but there was something in her past he knew, that had made her so distrusting, but tonight as well as being hurt he felt angry. Unbeknown to him he still wasn't fully aware of what Sadie was capable of and the only distraction for him as he lay on the hotel bed was a text message from Mia.

'Hey you. I'm all packed can't wait until the morning, shall we share a cab?' Mia.

Lucian was unsure whether it was because he was angry with Sadie that the realisation that Mia may actually be flirting with him was somewhat now obvious. Maybe he had dismissed it before, the whispering and sniggering in the office that sometimes took place when himself and Mia were together that had now somehow become more apparent. He liked Mia, yes she was an attractive woman, she was also clever and honest, as far as he knew, and she just seemed like a nice person and in the mood he was in and his anger towards Sadie, his text reply to her may have hinted a slight flirtation too, which in normal circumstances would be unprofessional and totally out of character for him.

'I'm looking forward to spending some time away with you too.' L.

Chapter Twenty-three

Summer solstice

'Congratulations for what Cassy?'

'Louie is your son; you have a son, ask your lovely girlfriend Sadie!'

'What? Sadie? What do you mean Sadie what does Cassy mean Louie is my son!?'

Kyle froze and waited for one of them to speak, his own voice was lost for a moment at the shocked words that he was hearing from his girlfriend. He looked at Cassy in horror and then back at Sadie, it was *his* nephew that they were talking about after all.

Sadie burst into tears; she knew that she could lose Lucian for good.

'I.... just want to talk to Lucian in private.... please?' She sobbed.

'Hang on this is my nephew we are talking about; I need to hear this too!' Kyle wasn't budging and neither were the others.

'Sadie I think it's a bit too late for secrets, just tell me, tell me what you have done!' Lucian shouted.

'Lucian I'm so sorry I really am I made a mistake okay, I fixed the D.N.A results, I arranged to have a copy made stating that you weren't the father to Louie, my hormones

were everywhere, you were threatening to leave me
and...' 'What? No, I don't believe I am hearing this;
please tell me you are joking Sadie!? You are not though
are you, oh my god you have really crossed the line
Sadie. I mean, I knew you were low, but this is really
low, even for your standards!' Lucian rubbed his hands
through his hair in dismay. 'I am shocked mate I mean...'

'Unbelievable, jeez what a low thing to do Sadie, you
have deprived my nephew of his biological father for the
last few years, are you fucking kidding me?' Kyle could
not believe what he was hearing. The others stood there
open mouthed. There was shocked silence for a few
moments and a lot of heads shaking until Kyle raised the
question to an usually quiet Cassy.

'Did you know about this Cassy? How long have you
known about Louie?'

'A while.' Cassy shrugged in a matter-of-fact tone as
she perched herself on the garden table peeling a label
from a beer bottle nervously. Lucian wasn't the only one
shocked at her casual attitude. 'Can you not sit on the
garden table please Cassy?' He snapped.

'A while? How long is a while Cassy? He is my
nephew for fucks sake, and you are my girlfriend I need
to know how long you knew about this vile behaviour
from your mate Sadie?'

'I said a while, I'm sorry to you both, I tried to tell you
at one point, but it was hard I couldn't because...'

'Hang on, who made the copy? Please don't tell me you
had anything to do with it Cassy?' Lucian and Kyle were
horrified at her reply. 'I'm so sorry I really am.

'Wow.' Alora was shaking her head, 'just wow.'

'Wow, what Alora?, Wow fucking what? Little miss perfect, I thought you'd be happy you can have Kyle now can't you? We all know that's what's been going on, with you Kyle and for those that didn't, well now you do!'

'Hang on a minute…'

'Cassy what the fuck is actually wrong with you, this is about you and her,' Kyle pointed to Sadie who was sitting quietly, on the garden chair with her head down in shame, 'and my nephew and the lies and depriving Lucian of his own son!'

'I knew you'd stick up for princess Alora, Kyle and what about you Blake, well did you know how your princess Alora has been having it away with my boyfriend?'

Blake needed a drink and went to the outside fridge and grabbed a beer.

'No Blake you don't need a drink, come on just don't, it's not worth it.' Alora begged. Blake raised his elbow towards Alora without touching her in a 'leave me alone' kind of way.

'I think I do need a drink! I want to hear this please?' Blake asked looking at Cassy.

'Oh no, don't just ask me, Sadie knows all about this too, she is the one with the pictures, or have you deleted them ones Sadie?' Cassy asked sarcastically.

Sadie had nothing to lose anymore and scrolled down to her phone and revealed a photo of Alora and Kyle standing at the entrance of the 'The Royale Hotel in West London. The name of the hotel was clear for all to see on the photo.

'There you go enjoy each other won't you and for the record Lucian, I am so sorry about Louie.' As Cassy started to leave, she knew that there was no going back, and that was the end of her and Kyle, her employment with Lucian and her friendship with Alora. It was time for a change, she had no choice, and she was fed up with living a lie.

'Hang on Cassy, I need to know more, how come you know so much about Alora and Kyle and how did you not say anything before? And you Kyle I will deal with you in a minute!' Blake shouted as he followed Cassy through the side garden gate, followed by Alora and Kyle.

'Cassy you have got it all wrong I'm telling you.' Alora shouted behind her.

'Go away the lot of you, and don't act innocent in all this Kyle, it was obvious from the word go you wanted Alora, you just settled for me cos she was with Blake!'

Blake, Alora and Kyle followed Cassy as she marched through the side gate out onto the street. Blake suddenly grabbed Alora and held her back as Cassy continued to march off down the lane.

'Let her go!' Kyle demanded, as Blake stood back he asked Alora and Kyle why Sadie had a photo of them both standing outside The Royale Hotel in the West End.

Mia was making Lucian a coffee, as he was trying to get hold of his ex-girlfriend Lisa, she wasn't answering. He wanted to speak to her as soon as he could, he wanted to be part of Louie's life, in the meantime he told Sadie to pack her things and go and stay at her parents' house. She followed his orders and waited patiently for the taxi, sobbing in the street. She knew she had really messed up big this time as tears rolled down her cheeks.

'Ah do you know what Blake just do one, that Sadie one is trouble, Kyle said as they all watched Sadie get into the taxi, 'look at what she has caused, if she is capable of denying a small boy of his father then she is capable of anything, and **Cassy, I will pack your things that you have left at mine and get them delivered, stay away from mine and leave the puppy too!'** Kyle shouted down the lane just before Cassy turned the corner. He was hurt, hurt for Louie, hurt for his sister, hurt for Lucian even, family was important to him and so was loyalty. It had been a new low from Sadie, but Cassy going along with the fake D.N.A results and helping that mental Sadie one, that was a shocker, he knew she didn't like kids, but he also realised he hadn't really known Cassy at all. This was unforgiveable, himself and Cassy as far as he was concerned were over.

'Can you all please be quiet! I have very young children trying to sleep! I will call the police if this carry's on!' Shouted a voice from the front door opposite from a rather large red-haired lady, who was heading towards them pointing her finger. As she got closer she resembled a much older middle-aged lady that appeared to be too old to still be bearing children. Her angry facial expression appeared to show that she may well go through with her threat and call the police.

Blake was aggressively moving towards Kyle and the middle-aged lady wasn't going anywhere, so Alora calmy apologised to her for the noise and pleaded with Blake to calm down.

Blake sighed heavily with clenched fists, as he looked at both Alora and Kyle, he hadn't even noticed anything between them before, but now he did notice something. Something deep, it was unbearable. Part of him wanted to kill Kyle, and part of him wanted to leave them to it, he wanted to know what had been going on.

He jumped into his car, he had only had two sips of beer, so he was able to drive, he waited for Alora to join him and opened the passenger window as the scent of Alora's perfume hit him hard.

He decided he wanted her with him, he wanted Alora to go back to his house so he could get to the bottom of everything.

'Okay sorry,' he tried with a false sense of calm, come on get in let's go.' He bossed. Alora stood there unresponsive staring at Blake as if he had two heads.

'No Blake, I am not getting in that car with you, please just go home.' Blakes face dropped. Kyle was relieved for Alora, he didn't trust Blake one bit, he had seen how frightened Alora had been of him at times, however this time she seemed different, stronger, as if it wasn't fear that had stopped her from going into Blakes car, more so that she had finally come to her senses, Kyle thought. Blake didn't even try to persuade her and put his foot down hard on his accelerator and drove off at a speed.

Mia received another apology from Christie, *'hey babe*

sorry I didn't realise the time; is the party swinging do you want me to join you when I'm done? Sorry I missed your call I'm still up to my neck in work.' She looked at her phone to reply, she was tempted to call a taxi and go to Christie's, Lucian was still on the phone to his father, and she wasn't really sure whether he wanted her to hang around or if he was just being polite, everyone else appeared to have left and there was now just the two of them. She stared at her phone for a while until Lucian interrupted her thoughts.

'It's getting colder now; do you want to come in? Thanks for the coffee but I could do with one of these now.' It was more like a statement than a request as he stood there waving a bottle of red in one hand and holding two wine glasses in the other. He looked broken, Mia thought, how she could refuse?

'Hey, no worries, I'm probably going to call it a night soon, see you in the week x' sent to Christie.

Christie was fifteen years older than Mia, and as well as being an incredibly rich and successful businessman, he was a very good looking one too. He was newly divorced with three teenager daughters, and according to his ex-wife she finally divorced him because he had been 'married to his work,' she was right, Mia agreed.

The taxi arrived as the curtain opposite twitched. Alora noted as she climbed in the back, Kyle took a seat as the front passenger.

'Where to mate?' Kyle turned around to face Alora, 'I want to pop round to Lisa's and speak to her face to face,

I have texted her and she's expecting me, will you come with me please, I could do with some morale support?' Alora didn't hesitate. 'Of course, she replied as she noted that she had just 6% battery left on her phone, she was relieved that there wasn't any missed calls or messages from Blake, surprisingly.

Cassy took a breather and leant against the old church wall. The clock chimed eight times and she looked at her watch to compare accuracy. It *was* exactly 8 o'clock. The night sky still light albeit the air a bit fresher. She had just under a mile to walk to her brother Theo's house. She really needed some things from Kyle's tonight; however, she couldn't face it. She had messaged Theo to see if she could stay at his and Chloe's for a few days, she would have to borrow some clothes from Chloe for work she supposed until the thought of work filled her with dread. Could she actually face Lucian on Monday? Would she still have a job?

She suddenly felt so ashamed but justified that the truth really needed to be told, hopefully when things have calmed down, she would explain herself as to why she had done what she had. She felt numb as she sat on the corner of the road, however her life needed a change and today was the first day for it., but first she had to message Lucian as she was due to be involved in a huge promotion on Tuesday, and she was sure he would still want her to be there. After two attempts to message him, she finally decided to put it off until tomorrow, and as she walked the evening streets of summer solstice, it really did feel like the longest day of the year.

The affair

Her
She felt his voice all the way through her body as he whispered softly to her. It was the first time she had entered his bedroom. She was sitting on *his* bed next to him. She loved the calming effect he had on her. His mouth was strong yet as soft as silk as his lips kissed her bare shoulders as he undressed her. He slowly moved her backwards onto his bed and undressed her until she was completely naked. She lay there vulnerable yet safe, she felt relaxed and yet intense, his hands so strong and yet with the softest touch he stroked her body. He teased her with his tongue and yet gave her so much pleasure. He took complete control and she let him.

Him
He had nothing to lose.

Present The Driver

'It was an accident, I was trying to save her, save her from everything including herself.'

Wilson tilted his head slightly to the right and looked at the man in front of him. He believed every word he had said, and what a shame it all was. He must be getting soft in his old age, he thought as he rubbed his chin. This man clearly loved Alora, and whether she was aware of that was another story. He had been honest and that was something, however, he had still committed a crime and would now have to face the consequences.

Would Alora ever forgive him? Only time would tell.

Alora

I knew it was time. Time to go back to life. I thought I had a choice, but obviously not, I mean, I wanted to go back at some point, but I would have preferred just a little longer time here with Johnny. He was now gone, he hadn't said goodbye, it was like deja vu all over again as he rode off into the sunset on horseback. I had tried to catch up with him and I rode for miles until I found myself back here at the bright light, although he did leave a dahlia here for me, I knew that was Johnny, he was the only one that knew it was my favourite flower and, I will fondly remember our last moments together, that's if I do remember, I hope so, until we meet again. At least I got a hug from Aunt Ede on the way back.

'Until we meet again pet.'

'Goodbye Aunt Ede love you, goodbye Johnny love you too, wherever you are.' Alora said as she sat underneath the pretty pink cherry blossom tree.

Alora passed the never-ending azure of blue, including geranium and hydrangea to the left of her and the expanse of green, orange and gold to the right side of her, where an ever-lasting bed of marigolds lay and as she was pulled back through the tunnel's bright light she left the beautiful array of colour until finally passing the stern looking lady holding the 'Heaven only' sign. She took a deep breath and opened her eyes. 'Hello Alora, welcome back, I am Detective Jenkins, and this is my colleague Detective Wilson.

Life is a journey.

Chapter Twenty-four

Previously on Monday, one day before the accident…

'**Ouch you bastard!**' Blake shouted in temper as he pulled his burnt hand away from the vehicle he was working on. His employee Jack had noticed he was in a foul mood today already and they had barely been working for an hour.

'Go and run it under the cold tap mate, I will put the kettle on and make a coffee.' Jack tried.

Blake had been so proud of himself; he hadn't messaged Alora at all yesterday let alone tried to call her, however late last night he gave in to temptation.

This morning he had been disappointed and angry to have not received even a text message from her. He had messaged her again regarding her car being picked up later today and she hadn't even bothered to reply, he thought angrily, and now he was trying not to imagine that she was with *him* last night, Kyle, as he put his hand under the tap of cold running water. He heard Devon pull up to work and he would try and get as much information out of him as possible, he was after all, Lisa's boyfriend, and Blake had suspected that Kyle would be visiting Lisa at some point, however Devon was giving nothing away.

Mia sensed the awkwardness in the office and unfortunately for Lucian and Cassy, as did Katrina. 'Cassy had arrived at 11am and had sat with Lucian in his office, and she's still in there now forty-five minutes later and Lucian has just called Mia in too and he is in a really serious mood!' Katrina was whispering to all that would listen.

'So, under the circumstances, I will give you a month to find another job, I will give you a good reference as discussed as professionally you have been great, however…'

'It's okay Lucian I know, and again I'm sorry.' She wasn't going to make matters worse today, she was grateful that she was still able to work for at least another month, although she may not still be around for that long.

'Okay, Lucian sighed as he placed his pen towards his mouth, his expression lightened as he swung his chair around to face Mia. 'So, if you could organise the advert etc to replace Cassy and arrange for the training of the new starter Mia, and if you could contact the agency today please, that would be great, thank you. Right, as discussed it's the big event tomorrow and I know you will be leaving us, but I am hoping you will still remain professional Cassy as there is some big names staying at the hotel where we are promoting and..'

'Yes of course, I will do my best Lucian.' Cassy

replied. Lucian sighed with relief and directed his open palm towards the door as a signal for Cassy to leave the room. She thanked him again on her way out. She needed a coffee, and she didn't know if she could stand the sexual tension between Lucian and Mia any longer anyway. She felt Katrina's eyes on her as she walked past reception towards the kitchen area and gave Katrina a sarcastic smile on her way past, she couldn't help herself. For the rest of her days working here she would continue to work hard and remain professional she decided. It was ten minutes before the end of her working day that Cassy started searching the internet. After opening her mother's profile, she started her search for flights to Australia.

Alora had contacted Blake from work, and she had told him that her phone was broken. His relief was short lived however, when she notified him that she wanted a full weeks break, no phone calls no messages no meetings, no contact and she just wanted one week to think about what *she* wanted. 'Don't you mean *who* you want not *what* you want?' had been Blake's quick reply, which he regretted as soon as he had said it.

'That's the lot.' Kyle muttered to himself as he dropped all Cassy's belongings onto Theo's doorstep. He didn't want her near him or near his house. He was pleased that Cassy's car hadn't been there, he thought as he headed home to prepare his house for his new visitors arriving from Ireland tomorrow, he couldn't be doing with any more drama.

Blake had remained as calm as he could all day, he had thrown himself into work and had almost completed the work that needed doing on Alora's car, the three things it had failed on, even though other customers had been waiting, including Javon, who never booked his car in the garage, he was one of those that would just turn up and say he needed it sorting a.s.a.p and only wanted Blake to work on it, him being the manager, even though two of his employees had more experience than Blake. He would try bribery with money and once had even offered Blake cocaine, which Blake had refused. He had dabbled a little when he was younger and had used it again after he had split from his ex-wife Ann, but on the whole he remained drug free. It was time to call it a day, he would work on Javon's car in the morning, he thought and give Alora the space that she needed tonight, he decided and would go home cook, shower then bed.

Alora looked at the pile of marking in front of her, she was undecided whether to eat, shower and put her comfy clothes on, or start the marking now, until she remembered about her phone being at Lisa's so she decided to do a couple of hours now then perhaps get a taxi to Lisa's around seven to pick up her phone before Louie went to bed and to eat and shower later.

Kyle had started to give his house a clean, it had been hard work with Rolo, he wasn't quite toilet trained yet, but he was getting there, he thought as he tried to coax Rolo through the dog flap that he recently had fitted from his kitchen to his garden and Rolo loved this new game. Kyle wondered for a moment if Rolo missed Cassy at all but decided probably not as she hadn't bothered taking him out much even though the nights were still light and the weather had been okay, up until tonight's rain. He felt nothing for Cassy now, his family came first, and he had been pleased that Lucian and Lisa had both wanted Louie in Lucian's life.

'Well, we have visitors arriving tomorrow Rolo and you need to be on your best behaviour, is that okay do you hear me?' Rolo barked for Kyle to throw the ball in his reply. A couple of hours later the house was all ready for his visitors, there was just one thing he needed, another couple of plates, so he grabbed his car keys and popped out.

Blake had tried he really had, he had cooked his dinner had a shower and refrained from messaging Alora, however he just could not relax. There was no football on, and in his restlessness, he had decided to drive past her house at a speed, to avoid being seen. He decided to drive around the roundabout at the end of Alora's road and completed a U turn so he could drive past her house again. An oncoming vehicle caught his eye and then his stomach turned as soon as he recognised Kyle pulling into Alora's drive, which encouraged him to put his foot down hard on the accelerator in anger.

The affair

Within seconds of him answering the front door, she knew that she could give in. *'It is going to be hard, hopefully it's not.'* His eyes are smiling along with his pleasing mouth. The palm of his hand open in a directional and welcoming manner to enter his house.

She hears her rehearsed speech that she has mentally repeated to herself in her head, all day.

'I'm sorry, this can't go on anymore, it's over as of now and I am not coming in tonight.'

She lifts herself up to the top step on his doorstep and takes a deep breath. It's too late. He's not even discreet. He pulls her body towards him almost as if he knew what she has been rehearsing all day. She enters his hallway, just for him to at least close the front door, her back is up against the hall wall. His warm hands undoing her bra, before she can resist he is pushed up against her. The buttoned-up silk blouse she purposely wore now completely open. As his mouth caresses her neck, he takes off his shirt baring his manly chest and finds herself wearing nothing but her black lacy underwear. Within minutes she had given in to temptation.

'No, no, no, had dominated her voice into yes, yes, yes.

'This was not meant to happen. Not tonight. I was here to end it, for good this time.'

Present

Alora thanked the nurse for her cup of tea and admired the painting on the wall directly in front of her as she took a sip of it. Not only did she appreciate her drink, but she also vowed to never take the simple pleasures in life, such as a simple cup of tea or a painting on a wall for granted ever again.

She felt some discomfort and pain in her back at times which was soothed with pain killers. Her legs felt as if they had been sitting on a long flight and needed a stretch but other than that she felt okay, unusually refreshed, like she had been on holiday, like she had rested, to which of course she had. Mentally she felt strong and appreciative, she appreciated the cup of tea, she appreciated the care that she had received, and she appreciated the painting in front of her that resembled an open window looking onto a field, but most of all she appreciated being alive.

*Acknowledgment and appreciation
are your foundation.*

Chapter Twenty-five

Tuesday - The accident

Sadie hadn't found the strength to go to work yesterday, she had cried more tears than she had cared to remember since Saturday, but today she felt stronger, she had messed up big time. She was aware Mia and Lucian had been getting close, she still had her little spy on her side, however *she* was the mother of his child and he had arranged to collect Amelia this evening and spend a few hours with her. He hadn't wanted any disruption for Amelia and had asked them both to stay the night and he had suggested for Sadie and Amelia to move back home, while he rented somewhere for a while. Sadie hoped and prayed that it wouldn't come to that. Lucian had an important work corporate event taking place today and tomorrow evening, he had arranged to meet Lisa after work, at the park so he could finally start to get to know his son Louie.

Blake was keeping Javon waiting, so he used his time to hang around and try and sell drugs to the staff and when he realised that Devon was seeing Lisa his ex-customer, he started asking questions about her as Lisa used to spend quite a lot of money on cocaine, plus he hadn't heard from her for a few years, however Devon responded with a very firm no thank you.

Cassy made a real effort to look the part and took a deep breath at her reflection. She had a big day ahead of her, and even though she was leaving the company she would still remain one hundred percent professional. She had shed a few tears on Sunday evening after Kyle had left most of her belongings on the doorstep, however she just told herself that she was happy before he came along and would be so again. She admired her reflection, not bad she thought in her new scarlet red dress.

Lucian arrived early at the office; his corporate event was starting at midday at the Marston Hotel in Central London he was going to take the tube today. He messaged Cassy to check that she was going to be there for 11 am as was he, she replied and confirmed that she wouldn't let him down. He managed to work a couple of hours and as he was leaving he noticed a walk-in customer enquiring about one of his hire cars, Katrina the receptionist was looking after her. The lady was a very tall lady and was also very well dressed in a matching cream mac and hat. Lucian was in a rush so his usual welcoming and thorough paperwork procedure, unbeknown to him would not be completed in his absence today as it normally would.

Blake was in a foul mood again, Alora's car could wait he thought angrily, he had carefully planned to still be working on it when she arrived.

Javon was pleased that his bribe had worked and that he

didn't have to hang around the garage today. He was a busy man and had people to see and drug deals to do.

Cassy didn't think she was going to be as nervous as she was as she started to prepare for her speech and the hotel started to fill with businessmen and women alike. She observed Mia, she seemed to be a natural and it made Cassy feel even more nervous, especially regarding her public speaking. Cassy had been a very shy child initially, even though no one believed a word of it when she had told them. She had been an extremely competitive child at school, always winning in sports day and dancing competitions, she had craved the attention of an audience when she was picked for pantomime at Christmas, however, public speaking turned her into nervous wreck, and she could feel butterflies in her tummy already. She wasn't due to speak for at least another hour and there was only one thing for it, to hit the bottle. The lady behind the bar seemed quite cute and their innocent chat soon became flirty. She'd had enough of men she thought, it was time to go back to women.

Kyle had welcomed his cousins into his home, they had all hit it off immediately, sharing a similar sense of humour too. Why they hadn't met before this day was questioned, however after a while Kyle felt like they had all known each other for years. What else was there to do on his rare day off other than to take them into London town and hit the pubs, they were Irish after all. His Aunt Maggie was due to join them in a few days.

Alora rang Blake's garage to see if her car was ready and luckily for her, Devon answered the phone. He told her it was still on the ramp and that Blake was working on it, Blake however had given out strict instructions that if Alora was to ring they should pass him the phone at once, as he was aware that she would ring his office number rather than his mobile. Devon had forgotten this and had told her Blake would ring her when her car was ready. With Kyle being off today, she decided that she would take a slow walk after work anyway, by then it should be ready. The day was drier and sunnier than yesterday, and she would cut through the park.

Lucian was pleased with Cassy's promotion she had remained professional, and all was going well. Mia was fantastic as usual, and he recalled the last time he was at this hotel at Sadie's 30th, it was a shame what she had done, as he really had fallen for her, but he was still hurt, hurt, shocked and angry, but tonight he was seeing Amelia and would pick her up after work, so he stayed clear of alcohol, however he noticed that Cassy had started to sway on her feet, thanked her for the day but urged her to drink a coffee or at least eat some nibbles.

It was 4pm and Kyle's cousin Laoise which was pronounced (Lee sha) had drank a little too much at O'Neill's in central London, and luckily for her, her brother had offered to drive them all home, Kyle had suggested the tube however his cousin wasn't keen on the tube, she had had a bad experience previously. Kyle, on the other hand, would rather walk than sit in London's traffic, as he knew all the side streets and short cuts. After a few rounds, he finally got them all home ready to meet Louie. Kyle hadn't stopped talking about him all afternoon and they couldn't wait to meet him. The last time Kyle had seen his Aunt Maggie was at his mums funeral, he was just seventeen at the time and it had all been a bit of a blur, Lisa was just sixteen and all the adults seemed to look the same, he recalled, and they had all offered himself and Lisa a home until 'they sorted themselves. ' At one point he had been tempted to move to Ireland where his grandparents were, but he decided there and then that he would work and provide for him and Lisa. He took any job he could, mainly pot washing and bar work and Lisa took a cleaning job and would baby sit for the locals, eventually Kyle bought out his sister Lisa until she found a flat and started her college training, around the same time Kyle started working as a teacher at Waverly.

Cassy sat on the bench for a rest and watched the young couple in front of her throwing the ball to their exceedingly small dog. Cassy wasn't sure of its breed; it was a bright rusty like fox colour and it made her think of Rolo. She hadn't paid him as much attention as she had wanted to, but she knew in her heart that her and Kyle wouldn't last, not after she had helped Sadie, hence why she hadn't wanted to get to attached to him. She envied the young happy couple in front of her and realised what a mess her own life was. Whether it was the daytime drinking, the thought of Rolo, or deep regret that caused the flood gates to open, it happened, there and then. She cried and cried for a good few minutes, muttering to herself, *'what a mess, what a total mess,'* between her sobs. Until she looked up and saw a familiar figure walking towards the bench, it was Alora.

'Yes I'm a mess Alora and you know what? I am sorry, I'm sorry for everything.'

'Cassy, what are you doing here, why are you not at work, what's wrong?' Alora asked as she sat next to her on the bench and caringly touched Cassy's arm.

'Alora, you have it all, a job you love, a house, a family and the love of Kyle, and me, I have lost Kyle, my job in a months' time…., I barely have a family, only my brother and he doesn't want me living with him and ..'

'Cassy, surely it's not that bad and listen to me number one, I don't have the love of Kyle I….'

'Come on Alora, I am not that stupid, please don't even try to deny you and Kyle to me, please, come on let's be honest shall we,' Cassy's voiced raised as she stood up and fiddled with placing her phone in her handbag and almost walked into a passer by jogger.

'Cassy come on, listen to me, sorry about that,' Alora apologised to the jogger.

'Listen to you Alora, always apologising, why what for? What are you apologising for? It's not your fault Kyle fell in love with you, and please don't insult my intelligence, 'hiccup'.. because you and I both know, come on Alora be honest I said, if Kyle had loved me like he loves you and even if any man would have loved me in the way that they loved you and, well now I am going to tell you something to put you in your place princess Alora………..'

Alora had never slapped anyone in the face before in her life, but Cassy had pushed her and pushed her until she had finally snapped.

'Wow, wow you don't like the truth do you Alora? Go on go running off, has it sunk in now, **finally!'** Cassy shouted as Alora marched off angrily.

'Me and you Cassy Reynolds are done!' Alora had heard enough now.

Blake rubbed his hands together proudly as he observed Alora's car, it was all ready for her, full M.O.T and service as new. He stood back and leant on the car next to Alora's and sipped his coffee, looked at his watch and noted that she should be here soon any time.

Kyle introduced Lisa and Louie to his cousins, and they played and sang with him. Louie asked why they all talked funny, and Kyle explained that they were from 'a place called Ireland across the water' and he promised Louie that he would take him there one day.

Alora arrived at Blake's garage and was very abrupt with him when she noticed him smirking at her, he was not to be trusted, she thought to herself. He was up to something; she couldn't quite put her finger on it, but her instincts were usually right.

Lisa noticed two missed calls on her phone as she went to take a photo of Louie with their new family, she was pleased of how things were finally falling into place. Firstly, meeting Devon, he was lovely and had a real calming influence on Lisa, he was great with Louie and worked hard at Blake's garage. She felt happy and secure for the first time in a while. Secondly, the fact that the truth had finally come out about Louie's father, she realised it wasn't his fault, as she had told Devon recently 'after what that bitch Sadie had done,' however she was happy for Lucian to be a part of Louie's life. She no longer had a drug habit; she had stopped as soon as she had found out that she was pregnant.

She had been mortified initially, it had been a scary thought, having to raise a baby alone, however, now she realised Louie was the best thing that had ever happened to her, and she was thoroughly enjoying motherhood, and with their extended family from Ireland, she finally felt like her, Louie and Kyle were all part of a family.

'Sorry Devon I can barely hear you, they are having a sing song in here, let me go in the garden.' Lisa said.

Kyle was in the kitchen talking to his cousin, there was a seriousness edged across both of their faces Lisa noted, however what she had just heard from Devon was also serious enough too.

'Kyle come here please,' Lisa waved Kyle to the garden from her kitchen.

'What's up?'

'Devon just rang me, seriously, he reckons Blake has

done something to Alora's car, and there is a guy called Javon..'

'Hang on what do you mean he has done something to Alora's car?'

'I don't know but he said it could be dangerous and this guy Javon he.... he used to be my drug dealer' she whispered, 'and Devon tried to stop Alora apparently, but a customer turned up and blocked him in and she drove off, he's rang her but no answer and ..'

'Okay well, we need to get down there quick, I've had a drink now though and so have you, let me think I will see if one of these can drive and we will try and get to her.

Present - London Borough Hospital

Alora had enjoyed the visit from her mum this morning and Suzi this evening, she had also had a very productive day attending physio. She thought about the last few days. She had tried to explain to her mother that she had seen Johnny, however when her mother had cut her off in the nicest possible way, telling Alora she had been dreaming, Alora decided to keep her 'journey' as she called it to herself. She had opened up to Johnny and spent hours with him and had a ball, she had died and gone to heaven, but she knew no one would believe her, her time spent with Johnny was precious, her time on the farm was fun, but most of all she had gone through the last through years of her life and Johnny had made her see what was most important in her life. Johnny had

Alora her worth.

Aside from what Johnny wasn't aware of Alora's mind was made up and she deserved to be treated better. Alora had had given Blake her love, time, and patience, encouraged him, gave up a lot of her friends, and had received little in return.

She was just about to start her new book given to her by Suzi when there was a tap on her room followed by the visit she had been expecting.

'Hello Alora,' Alora observed the two police officers standing in front of her, both of them not dressed in a police uniform but it was obvious to her, who they were, and she replied a quiet 'hello' back.

'I am Detective superintendent Wilson, and this is my colleague Detective superintendent Jenkins.'

'Okay'

'So, how are you feeling Alora?' asked Jenkins.

'I am very well, thank you.' Alora replied putting her book face down onto her bed.

'That's good, now, we are going to have to take a statement from you,' Wilson said carefully, 'do you recall anything about the accident at all?'

'No, not really just that I was hit head on as I was turning right and that was it, the next thing I remember is waking up here, the nurses have all explained that I have had an operation on my back and the physio and…'

'Okay, do you remember writing this letter that was found in your car?' Wilson handed the envelope to Alora, and she unfolded the A4 lined paper and began to read.

'Dear Blake, I want to first apologise for all the pain and misery I have caused you, so sorry. It started off as a silly little kiss and went on from there. I didn't plan for this to happen, I didn't plan to fall in love with Kyle, however like I said it just happened and I am truly sorry. I don't think me and you are meant to be together, I know you tried very hard but I could not make you happy. I hope you find the happiness that you deserve I really do. Lots of Love Alora.'

P.S I am truly sorry.

The accident continued...

Alora tears were rolling down her cheeks as she bashed the steering wheel, the bearded guy to the left of her at the traffic lights was looking at her strangely. She hadn't noticed and she hadn't cared. She took another swig of the coffee that Blake had left in the car for her from the star bucks around the corner, which he always treated her to when she visited his garage. It tasted disgusting and she felt sick, but she was thirsty, so she drank the rest while waiting at the never-ending traffic lights. Pushing her foot down onto the brake was becoming a problem, as she tried to use what little strength she had, ignited by her fury after Cassy's outburst, to push down harder on the brake. She thought of Kyle and how one little kiss that was meant to be a peck on the cheek had turned into what it had. She thought of the guilt that she had felt as she had responded in a split second to that kiss. She thought about how she was prepared to tell Cassy about it when it had happened, but she hadn't because she never wanted to hurt her friend. She thought about how prior to that silly kiss, she had been good to Cassy and how she had always been there for her, yet Cassy had given her so much grief and made her feel worthless after she had offered Cassy a roof over her head. She had given her advice and had treated her like the little sister that she had never had.

She couldn't differentiate between whether she was swaying, or her car was, as her head felt heavy, the lorry in front of her was suddenly a blur and she felt herself trying to drive to the woods, she knew she didn't want to go home. Her eyes felt heavy as she approached the junction, and it took all her strength to flick on her indicator as she waited to take the right turn to the woods. As the black car hit her she saw a familiar face until she was looking down at herself in the hospital.

Chapter Twenty-six

Present London Borough Hospital

'No, I definitely did not write that letter; it looks similar to my handwriting but it's not mine.'

'Okay we have analysed the writing,' Wilson said as he folded the letter back up and put it in his pocket.

'I don't understand who would …'

'Okay we will have to take a formal statement from you soon, but for now,' Wilson paused as he looked at Jenkins and she nodded back at him, 'we now have the driver of the other vehicle that hit your car and I can tell you that ..'

'Morning Alora, oh excuse me officers but Alora still needs to rest for a while, I know you are doing your job, but she has had a busy day with her physio and visitors,' the nurse interrupted in her caring manner.

Wilson handed Alora his card and told her that they would be back soon, there was something very warm and caring about him Alora noted as he urged her to rest and then whispered something to the nurses as he left. Alora's started to overthink and remembered what Johnny had told her about overthinking and picked up her book, after a couple of chapters she fell into a deep sleep.

'That will be £44.20 please love.'

'Take £50 thank you.'

'Thanks very much and good luck on your new venture.' The taxi driver took the suitcase out of the boot of the car and it all now seemed so real for Cassy as she headed towards the terminal at Heathrow airport. With an eagerness to leave the country she had arrived a few hours earlier than she had needed to for her flight to Sydney Australia, the terminals sometimes confused her, so she had relied on the taxi driver to take her to the correct place. She liked the excitement of airports and decided to have a wander around before checking in and found herself at arrivals. She liked to people watch those arriving in England and would make up her own scenario of what their lives would be like and wonder if it was their first time here. She had focused her attention on a young girl that was excitedly being welcomed by what could be her mother and father as they hugged her tightly. As she lit her cigarette, Cassy wondered if she would receive such a welcome by her mother at the airport who had arranged to pick her up when she landed.

Deana set her alarm in the hope that she would sleep well tonight, the last few nights she had barely slept at all as the thought of meeting her daughter for the first time had overwhelmed her emotions. She had been delighted when Cassy had contacted her asking if she could stay with her for a while, albeit she was extremely nervous to see her daughter again after almost thirty years. Her baby Cassy was now a woman, and she was only in her mid-forties herself. She had wrongly assumed that Sean her husband would be against the idea at first, however he had surprised her with his reaction and told her that Cassy could stay as long as she liked. Sean was aware of the pain and heartache that Deana had suffered being made to leave her baby daughter in the UK, which had caused a rift between her and her parents especially after the births of their other children. Deana was lucky that Sean earned enough money so that she never had to work, albeit she was a full-time mum to three young children, one girl and twin boys, and she was hoping that Cassy would bond with them as she had some fun days out as a family planned along with some mother and daughter's days too. She switched off her lamp and wondered about Cassy and her life and knew that this time tomorrow evening she would be on her way to be reunited with her baby girl.

'Is this your lighter dear?' Cassy thoughts were interrupted by the petite dark haired Irish lady that had just bent down to pick up Cassy's lighter.

'Oh yes thank you.' Cassy replied as she noticed what a kind face the petite Irish lady had and wondered whether she was visiting England or lived here already. She was travelling alone and was wheeling a small old fashioned mustard coloured suitcase and was wearing a long thick grey coat that appeared to be in Cassy's mind an Irish tweed. She watched as the lady crossed herself before taking the crossing towards the taxi rank. As Maggie got into the taxi she said a quiet prayer for her family here in England. Kyle had offered to pick her up, but she had declined, she knew he had enough on his mind.

Kyle sat in his car at the car park at the hospital unsure of which one out of the two to visit first. He needed to see them both, the driver and Alora. He sat there for a few minutes until his thoughts were interrupted by what he was now witnessing. He breathed a sigh of relief and inwardly smiled, 'finally' he muttered to himself as he observed what appeared to be Blake being arrested, 'justice at last.'

As Blake took his seat in the back of the police car he knew that it was time to finally admit the truth.

Kyle wandered through the hospital with mixed emotions, inwardly smiling at what he had just witnessed while also feeling slightly nervous.

***

Alora had attended physio this morning and had been told by the consultant that she was doing very well and would soon be able to go home. Physically, she was feeling good, mentally too, yet she still had lots of questions spinning around her mind. She thought back to her time with Johnny and how it appeared to seem so real, although at times she questioned herself as to whether the last week she had spent with him had all been a dream or had she really visited heaven while she was in her coma, either way she had loved how relaxed she had felt. The laughs she had had with Johnny and her discovery of nature and also her discovery of herself. Johnny had taught her, ironically she reflected, to enjoy life, slow down and to think of herself and he had also reminded her not to overthink, but most of all he reminded her that you do only get one shot at life. She didn't want to go back to the rat race and the mess that was part of her life before the accident, she had definitely re-evaluated her life and she had made her mind up about Blake. She thought about that letter and wondered why it was found in her car, until she heard Johnny's voice telling her not to over think and that the truth would be revealed, so she snapped herself out of it and noticed that it was visiting time. There had been one particular visitor that she had wished to see and as her door opened and Kyle stood there, her wish had come true.

Wilson had never seen Jenkins so excited he thought as he observed her acting in a child like way.

'I can't believe how easy this has been,' she beamed as they took a break and paused the interview for five minutes.

Blake had decided to finally tell the truth and admit everything, well almost, and now Jenkins was eager for him to admit that he drove the car.

Blake had surprised himself with his honesty during his interview, however he had now realised he had lost everything and felt that there was perhaps nothing more to lose. Deep down he knew somewhere there was a decent guy that had lost his way, plus Jenkins had told him that his honesty would pay off.

Firstly, he admitted to writing the letter that was found in Alora's car to himself addressed from Alora by stating that he simply wanted to keep up his pretence that he was the victim and he had wanted to hurt Alora. Next he admitted to putting drugs into Alora's coffee which had caused her reactions to slow down while she was driving prior to her accident. Afterwards he admitted to not fixing her breaks when testing her car for it's Ministry of Transport test because of his jealousy over his thoughts of Alora and Kyle which had made him extremely angry. Finally, he also admitted to planting cocaine into Alora's car supplied by Javon to 'set Alora up,' even though no trace of any drugs were actually found and also in his admission, he stated that he couldn't remember.

Jenkins could not hide the delighted look on her face.

'Hello Kyle.'

'Hi Alora,' Kyle smiled, yet his lovely green eyes appeared to not quite be smiling as much as Alora had remembered and something inside was telling her that she wasn't going to be happy about what she was about to hear. 'Hello stranger,' she beamed, nonetheless as she shuffled herself upright as Kyle seated himself on the chair next to her bed.

'So how are you feeling? Kyle's eyes brightened up for a moment Alora noticed.

'I am on the mend and feeling okay, I really am.'

'That's so good, glad to hear, and you are looking well.'

'So, what's been happening in your life?' Alora was all ears and welcomed any news, she knew Kyle and she knew he had something to tell her.

'Well...'

'What's been happening at work?' Alora instantly regretted her interruption.

'Ha, not a lot, they have had a temporary teacher in for you, but the kids have been asking after you every day and..'

'Bless them,' she interrupted again then mentally told herself to just listen.

'Alora, I have something to tell you and I want it to come from me,' Kyle rubbed his fingers back through his long wavey dark curls. 'Firstly, Blake has been arrested, I just saw him and two police officers literally in the car park at the front. I don't know what for well, that's a lie I know a few things that it could be, but I will let the police tell you more in detail.'

Alora was silent and waited patiently for Kyle to finish what he was saying.

'I know he had something to do with the accident, but like I said, I am sure the officers will be visiting you soon.'

'Okay,' Alora managed, she swallowed nervously and asked the main question that was spinning around her mind. 'Was he the driver, was he the one that hit my car and drove off?'

Cassy placed her hand luggage above her and then made herself comfortable, she was pleased she had the window seat as the aeroplane boarded its last few passengers. *'Goodbye England'* she thought as she reflected on what had been her life for the last few years as she finally felt some optimism. She wasn't running away, it was time to spend some time with her birth mother and her family, but most of all, she had been on a path of self-destruction for years and she had caused a lot of hurt and she knew it was time to grow up. She had been genuinely sorry for her actions, and she had apologised again and explained in the four letters that she had posted first class yesterday. One to Kyle apologising for her actions and the way she had treated his nephew Louie. One to Alora apologising for her actions and the things she had said to her in her drunken state at the park. One to Lucian apologising for her actions regarding his son Louie but also explaining that Sadie had actually blackmailed her into doing so. Her final letter had been sent to Blake.

Dear Blake

I just want to say that I really hope you sort yourself out, you really need to and so do I. I hope you get the help you need and its time to stop lying. Stop lying to yourself and everyone, please get the help you need. I am flying to Australia to meet my mother and her family and will be gone for 3 months at least.

P.S
I have told Alora about our affair, I told her everything.

Cassy

Blake had broken down in tears as he read the letter it had been the final straw. There was a realisation at what he had become. He had betrayed Alora, and he had listened to Sadie trying to convince himself and Cassy that Alora and Kyle were in love. He had played the victim and lied to Mr. Collins his psychiatrist and told him that Alora had physically hurt him including the coffee cup that *he* threw at Alora's mirror. He had buried the domestic abuse that he had suffered in the hands of his ex-wife Ann. It had been *her* that had physically and mentally abused him and instead of seeking help he had treated Alora how *he* had been treated previously. He had now lost the love of his life and he knew it. He pulled himself together and would visit Alora at the hospital and apologise profusely, if she would let him, and then he would go and hand himself in to the police, after he had visited Alora. He was surprised at how calm she had been. She had listened to him and whether it was her that rang the police after, or whether it was pure coincidence he would never know, however as he was leaving he was arrested by Detective Superintendent Jenkins and Wilson.

Kyle hadn't answered Alora's question.

'Was Blake the driver, was he the one that hit my car and drove off? It's okay I know everything else Blake came to visit me earlier and told me everything, he told me how him and Cassy had been having an affair all along, which Cassy had told me in the park, that's what I slapped her. Sadie had blackmailed Cassy by using a photo of her and Blake entering the Royale Hotel together, which was when she must have photographed us when we were following her. That clearly was why she had the picture of us two on her phone outside the Royale. Ironically, I always thought that if Blake was playing away it would be with Sadie, not Cassy. Blake also admitted not fixing my cars brakes properly when it had its M.O.T, spiking my coffee and planting a letter and a package of cocaine in my car.

Kyle's eyebrows rose as he listened to what Alora was telling him. 'Don't worry I have recorded it all on my phone, he didn't see me, I pressed record as he went to close the door. He told me he was going to hand himself in and I believed him, I assume the police got to him first. I called Wilson as soon as he left, but they must have been on their way anyway. Just one thing though he said he wasn't the driver, and I wasn't sure if he was telling the truth or not, oh and sorry to be the one to tell you that Cassy was cheating on you Kyle.' Kyle shrugged, Cassy cheating on him, currently seemed unimportant.

'No, he wasn't the driver Alora, bless you, you need to brace yourself for this.' Kyle sighed. 'I know who it was, but we were trying to help you we were trying to save you.

'What do you mean we? What do you know Kyle? Alora asked bemused. 'Well, Devon rang Lisa, he said there was a drug dealer that had been hanging around the garage his name was Javon, one of Lisa's old dealers, anyway Devon wasn't sure about your brakes, he didn't know about your coffee being spiked either, but he had seen Blake place a package in your car and guessed it was drugs. All we were trying to do was get to you and make sure you were okay and also take the drugs from you. I had been drinking with my cousin's over from Ireland, so my cousin took the hire car, which Laoise had hired from Lucian. I went in Lisa's car with her and we headed down to Blake's garage to try and follow your route. It was because of the cocaine that he left you after he hit you as you were turning into the woods. I'm so sorry Alora he waited until the ambulance arrived and I went to the hospital straight away and Johnny disposed of the drugs, but he was injured and …'

'Johnny?

'Yes Alora Johnny, my cousin. Johnny Bailey, I'm sorry.'

'Johnny Bailey, is he your cousin from Ireland?' Alora's face paled, 'Johnny Bailey?'

'Yes I had no idea that you and him even knew each other, let alone that you were together when you were younger it wasn't until we got talking and I mentioned an Alora that he realised who you were and...'

'Hang on, so Johnny is your cousin, and he is not dead?' Kyle looked at Alora strangely, 'No he's not dead, he was injured in the accident and was found unconscious, and they brought him in here, just down the corridor there. He has told the police everything, and... well he is gutted at what has happened but am telling you now Alora he was trying to save you and some how he knew you would be heading to the woods.

Alora was numb she had no words just mixed emotions and pure shock of what she was hearing, half elated that Johnny was still alive, shocked that it was *he* who had hit her car, and totally bewildered about her time with Johnny in the afterlife. It was all she could take in one day after Blake's and Johnny's visit and when the police arrived she told them that she knew everything and that she had had enough visitors for one day and that she had been discharged from hospital and would be in touch soon.

After Alora had packed all her belongings she looked around the hospital room, she was still in shock.

Blake had finally admitted the truth to himself, and everyone else. Alora felt slightly relieved after his admission and was looking forward to going back to some sort of normality, as normal as it could be after the last few weeks

As for Kyle, she knew he had feelings for her, and she had with him at some point. They hadn't been completely innocent and that photo of them kissing had been a one off, but it had happened, however, now with hearing what she had, the thought that her life would maybe now be simpler seemed ridiculous.

'Johnny though, wow,' she thought. It had totally thrown her, and the fact that he was Kyle's cousin. She had never questioned it or put two and two together, because her father had told her that Johnny had been killed in a motorbike accident. Kyle Bailey, Johnny Bailey, Ireland, it was only when he had contacted his Aunt Maggie, Johnny's mother that Kyle had mentioned his cousins from Ireland, plus Kyle had referred to Johnny as 'J ball.'

Alora's thoughts were interrupted, and her tummy tied in knots as her hospital room door opened.

'Hello Alora, what's the story?' Those emerald, green eyes were smiling, and she couldn't help the feeling of warmth in her heart. 'What's the story? What's the story? Johnny how long have you got!' Alora burst into tears.

'I'm sorry Lor I really am, please just let me explain before you over think, please just let me explain.

Fate

In a twist of fate.

Blake had finished work on time for once and as he popped his new shades on, the mid May sun was beating down on his face as he eagerly pulled on to the short dual carriageway drive to his home. He was both nervous and excited at the thought of his first date with Alora tonight. In his haste unbeknown to him, he had left his mobile phone at work. As soon as he had taken that left turning onto the dual carriage way, he knew that he should have driven the other way through the busy streets of London instead. Unbeknown to him, and half a mile in front, there had been a major lorry spill and he would be sitting on the dual carriage way for almost four hours.

Alora's dry sense of humour and her optimism would always let her see the funny side of what some would consider to be a disappointment or simply bad luck.

'Every cloud,' she muttered to herself as her eyes turned to her good-looking new colleague standing at the bar. 'Did you want ice Alora?'

'No thanks Kyle,' she beamed gratefully as her luck had turned around. Just five minutes ago she had been sitting alone waiting for her new date Blake, he had been over forty-five minutes late and she had texted him and had received no reply. She was about to leave when her new colleague Kyle Bailey had, by pure coincidence walked into the bar.

'Those green eyes,' she thought admiringly, they had

reminded her of her first love, Johnny, Johnny Bailey, she thought as she reflected to her teenage years and wondered whether it was true that he had been killed in a motor bike accident, according to her father.

Her thoughts were interrupted as Kyle placed her disaronno and coke in front of her and raised his glass of beer. 'Well, here's to getting stood up on your first date, Alora,' he laughed.

'Thanks,' Alora giggled, she liked him already, Kyle Bailey. As she raised her glass, she told Kyle that he reminded her of her first love Johnny.

'Well funnily enough, I have a cousin in Ireland called Johnny.'

True love stories never have endings, and the path of true love never runs smooth.

Hello readers, I hope you enjoyed Him, Her & that secret. The above was an example of how sometimes life can take a different route, when for example fate steps in. If Blake had taken an alternative route home and had not met Alora that day, the lives of those all involved would now be completely different.

Following on is the sequel titled, The Secret Love Triangle, where Alora will battle with her strong feelings for the two men in her life Johnny Bailey and Kyle Bailey, long distance and newly found cousin's.

The Secret Love Triangle is written in two parts.

Alora's path after Blake..

Alora hides her feelings for Kyle when he starts dating Jenna, a young teacher at the school, her slight pangs of jealousy leave her with mixed emotions and her love life becomes more complicated when Johnny moves to England after his prison sentence and begs Alora for forgiveness. Johnny tries desperately to encourage Alora to move to Ireland with him, while Kyle encourages her to stay in England and tensions start to arise between them all.

Alora's path without Blake…

Alora and Kyle have been living together for two years and are incredibly happy, until Johnny Alora's first love and Kyle's cousin visits them from Ireland. Alora's old feelings returns, which causes a conflict of emotions for all concerned. There was no Blake, there was no accident and Johnny and Alora hadn't seen each other for almost twenty years. Old feelings are evoked for both Alora and Johnny, where Alora's love life becomes complicated.

On both paths of fate for Alora she struggles to choose between those emerald eyes.

The Secret Love Triangle
The Sequel

Chapter One

'Jesus Christ, you can be stubborn can't you Lor, I just want two minutes, just two minutes please, or else I am going to sing the 'Fields of Anthenry' at the top of my voice all night, and all the next day and the next week after that, on your doorstep, naked!'

A tender smile spread across Alora's face momentarily. She had listened to Kyle; she had heard his attempted justification of the reason why Johnny had run off after his car had hit her and, she understood that Johnny was trying to protect her. She *had* forgiven him for the accident, what was there to forgive? It was an accident. She knew that Blake had planted drugs in her car, and she understood why Johnny had run off with the drugs package, however she still could not quite forget the fact that he had ran off, even now, one year on. There he was, now singing the 'Fields of Anthenry' at the top of his voice, he had followed through with his threat and Alora was tempted to let him in, just because she was embarrassed. It wasn't just about the accident as to why Alora wasn't ready to talk to Johnny yet, in her mind she had spent a wonderful few days with Aunt Ede and Johnny in heaven and it had given her the strength that she needed to change her life and begin and new chapter with a sense of rejuvenation. She hadn't wanted that feeling to end, although she was delighted Johnny was still alive, but she also wanted the time that she had believed to have spent with Johnny to be real and not just a dream. She had received a few letters from Johnny while he was in prison and she had tried to ignore them, but she hadn't been able to. He had served five months and had done his time, it had been one year to the day since she had been discharged from hospital, one year to the day that she had seen Johnny, and she had kept her promise to herself to remain single, completely single, not even a friendly date for one whole year.

'Okay Johnny, I give in,' Alora said to herself as she opened her front door to a singing smiling pair of emerald eyes.

Kyle passed Jenna the menu, he had broken his promise to himself to not date anyone from work. It wasn't really a date, he justified, Jenna had won a meal in the summer school fate raffle and her friend had 'let her down via text message' just as she was about to leave work, and when she mentioned it to Kyle he had offered to help her out. Kyle had looked at the menu distractedly and then noted the time, 7.36pm, he knew by now his cousin Johnny would be knocking on Alora's front door, which he had already planned on his flight. In Kyle's mind, with him reflecting back to one year ago, he had wrongly predicted that by now he would have been happily dating Alora as she was the exception to his rule of the promise to himself dating anyone from work, and they would be past the honeymoon period and starting to get serious. Instead, currently, he had his cousin Johnny staying with him, that was still insisting that he would not give up on his battle for Alora's forgiveness after what he had done. His cousin Johnny also had no idea of how Kyle felt about Alora, and Kyle was now torn between the woman that he secretly loved and his cousin. Kyle and Alora had become the best of friends, she was his only close female friend, and he was her only close male friend. Neither of them truly admitted their feelings for one and other and now with Johnny out of prison Kyle was torn between his family and Alora.

'The path of true love never runs smooth.' Kyle had heard his Aunt Maggie telling Johnny and Kyle could not have agreed more he thought as Jenna had tried to grab his attention.

Jenna was cute, smart, pretty, and a little bit younger bit than Kyle, he had no idea how much she fancied him, plus he had no idea how Jenna had tricked him into joining him at the meal she had won, between her and her best friend and colleague Kiera, they had hatched out their little plan to set up the winning raffle prize so that Jenna could go on what she saw as a date with Kyle.

'Earth to Kyle,' Jenna giggled as she played with her hair, 'are you having a starter or just a main.'

'Sorry Jenna I was miles away.'

Chapter Two

Alora's life without Blake

'Of course, I am not jealous that you are taking a younger, prettier lady out to dinner who also happens to be your work colleague and my ex-work colleague babe.'

The hint of sarcasm in Alora's voice was not wasted on Kyle.

'Younger, yes but definitely not prettier than you sweetheart.' Kyle confirmed as she flicked his towel at Alora before he wrapped it back around himself.

'Okay I believe you; you smell good though, do you want me to pick you a shirt and style you hair?'

'Go away, you can go in my place if you want, I'm knackered anyway, you know I was roped into it, but if you're getting jealous…'

'I'm only taking the P, you know that' Alora replied as she watched Kyle rub his thick dark curls as he hovered over his pastel shirts.

'Don't wear the green one though as it will clash with your eyes.'

'Honestly, I am knackered, do you want to text Jenna and go in my place?'

'No, I have yoga and anyway, we trust each other, just

make sure you come home for your dessert. I have got things to do here afterwards, especially as your cousin 'J ball' or whatever it is you call him is coming over from Ireland tomorrow.'

'Yep, should be fun, met him once as a kid, but he's a bit of a character I hear, anyway, yes if you could just check the spare rooms are tidy please love, that would be great.' Kyle smiled as he realised how lucky he was to have Alora.

Kyle and Alora had been living together for two years and it had been going very well. He had plans to propose in the summer holidays which was just a few weeks away. Kyle and Alora no longer worked at the same school as they had agreed working and living together would be too much, plus one year ago Alora had been head hunted to work as a deputy head mistress at a local girl's school, whereas Kyle remained at Boadfield Primary. Unbeknown to Kyle, Jenna his colleague knew more about Kyle than he thought, as she had been best friends with Ella, the sixth form student that Kyle had formed an intimate relationship with some years ago at Waverly secondary and with Jenna being newly single, she had grown even closer to Kyle as she started to confide in him. Kyle had no idea that she may have an ulterior motive other than his friendship.

'Right, I am off to yoga, see you later, be good!' Alora teased as she placed her yoga mat over her shoulder. She knew she did not have anything to worry about she thought, she would let this go as a one off considering that she had attended a business meal recently with the board of governors, and one of the parents her colleagues seem to all swoon over, 'Liam the looker' as he was known by some of the parents and Alora's colleagues. He had given Alora a lift home after as he wanted to pick her brains of the local future and further education for his children, albeit she already knew him, being the father of Kyle's sister Lisa's child Louie. Alora and Kyle adored Louie and they had both discussed and agreed that they would soon be hoping to be parents themselves in the not-too-distant future.

As the plane descended for landing, Johnny beamed as he gazed at the blue summer skies of London. Of course he was looking forward to seeing his cousin Kyle again after all these years, plus, after their last message where Kyle mentioned an 'Alora,' his heart had skipped a beat. Surely it couldn't be? He thought happily, hopefully it could. His first love, his Alora, the one who broke his heart as a teenager and the one who's heart he knew he would have broken after his sudden departure back home to Ireland, either way he would soon find out.

Those emerald eyes

Lost In Time
Lost In Travel
Him, Her & that Secret
The Secret Love Triangle 2022